Make Way for Her

Make Way for Her

And Other Stories

Katie Cortese

UNIVERSITY PRESS OF KENTUCKY

Scholarly publisher for the Commonwealth,
serving Bellarmine University, Berea College, Centre
College of Kentucky, Eastern Kentucky University,
The Filson Historical Society, Georgetown College,
Kentucky Historical Society, Kentucky State University,
Morehead State University, Murray State University,
Northern Kentucky University, Transylvania University,
University of Kentucky, University of Louisville,
and Western Kentucky University.
All rights reserved.

Editorial and Sales Offices: The University Press of Kentucky
663 South Limestone Street, Lexington, Kentucky 40508-4008
www.kentuckypress.com

These stories, sometimes in altered form, originally appeared in the following publications: "Sweetness on the Tongue" in *Blackbird* as "The First Necessary Heartbreak"; "Desire Comes Closer" in *Juked* as "Change Begins with You"; "Firebug" in *Carve Magazine*; "Welcome to Snow" in *Epiphany*; "Straight and Narrow" in *Willow Springs* as "International Cooking for Beginners"; "Bitter, Sweet, Salt" in *Zone 3 Literary Journal*; "The Bounce Back" in *Talking Writing* as "Flight Plan"; "Lighter, Bluer, Clearer, Colder" in *Passages North* as "Tug-of-War"; "Make Way for Her" in the *Baltimore Review* as "Wakulla Springs"; "Silent Blooms of Sudden Heat" in the *Doctor T. J. Eckleburg Review* as "Fort Lauderdale Is for Lovers."

Library of Congress Cataloging-in-Publication Data
Names: Cortese, Katie, author.
Title: Make way for her : and other stories / Katie Cortese.
Description: Lexington, Kentucky : University Press of Kentucky, [2018]
Identifiers: LCCN 2017045449| ISBN 9780813175126 (hardcover : acid-free
    paper) | ISBN 9780813175133 (pdf) | ISBN 9780813175140 (epub)
Classification: LCC PS3603.O78255 A6 2018 | DDC 813/.6--dc23 LC record
available at https://lccn.loc.gov/2017045449

For Robby

The lamb must learn to run with the tigers.
—Angela Carter, "The Tiger's Bride"

Contents

Sweetness on the Tongue

The writer's conference is a camp for grownups, a thing Lily is not yet, but her presence is tolerated since her mother is a famous poet, engaged to teach a workshop, and her father a journalist stationed in Alexandria, a port city north of Cairo famous for its destroyed library where last month another American journalist— someone her father claims not to have known—was killed in a violent protest. Lily doesn't know the details because he is careful not to share them during their Wednesday morning Skypes. He's safe, he says. Getting fat on hummus.

He'll come home soon, he says, the way he always does.

While her father documents Egypt's troubled democracy, Lily is toted to this medieval stronghold of a college in the wooded mountains of a southern state, herself toting little more than boredom and summer reading books, which grow fat with humidity. Last summer, while her father was in Syria with the BBC, she was toted to a cluster of cabins in a northern wood. The year before, it was a beach where her father spent three days before leaving for Malawi. That was the last time Lily remembers wearing a swimsuit without worrying over her thighs, which have recently begun to round and firm, taking on a womanly shape without her permission.

Lily can be toted places because she is fifteen, slight, a year

1

away from a four-wheeled independence, and because she is an obedient, agreeable girl. Most of her power comes from living out her vigorous youth, steadily growing into the beauty she knows she will become because she looks so much like her mother's old pictures.

Among the many lessons her parents have imparted is that everything comes down to dominance or its lack—nature abhors equality the same way it abhors a vacuum. For now, her mother is still beautiful, and for now, Lily is less so, but her mother plucks white from her mahogany hair each morning, and her jowls have begun to sag, though Lily would never tell her. Her parents have also taught her to practice kindness whenever possible, and she tries.

To compensate for this year's smallish stipends, workshop leaders are invited to campus a week before their eager students, a gesture billed as half vacation, half writing retreat. On the first, quiet mountain morning, Lily explores the grounds, waves to a young mother corralling twin boys across a quad, reads *Madame Bovary* until she falls asleep in the sun, and wakes on her bench to a sky so bluely radiant she thinks at first she's fallen into another dream.

Later, walking to the dining hall, fellow writers stop her mother with hugs and tell Lily the last time they saw her she was knee-high to a grasshopper, or still growing out of her baby fat, or just the cutest thing this side of the Mississippi. Again and again they ask, "And what about you, honey. Do you write too?"

Her mother answers for her. "Lil has eggs in lots of baskets," she says, prattling on about the swim team, piano, volunteering at the library, her excellent, uniform grades.

Lily does not say that she has begun to keep a notebook of small, insignificant observations, like the way her mother's fountain of curly hair sets her off like quotation marks, or how her nickname is a homonym to li'l, a synonym for less than. After dinner she will turn to a new page in her royal blue journal and write: "Grackles strut, throating false cries / dropping feathers that ink the ground black."

The second morning, at breakfast, Lily and her mother share a table with a young writer famous for his futuristic short stories, his wife Deanna—the woman from the quad, her hair an enviable shade of honey—a rail-thin playwright, and a wizened, shawl-wrapped woman Lily recognizes, a rock star insofar as poets can be. The writer of futuristic stories shakes her mother's hand with both of his. He admires her work, he says, it's an honor, just an honor. Lily's mother says he is sweet to say so. She says his reputation precedes him, which means she's being kind.

Lily sets down her plate. Pokes at her egg. It was foolish to hope the summer would be free of entanglements since there's always at least one new hangdog suitor. They bother Lily more than her mother, who says moving people toward love is the point of all she's done. The writer of futuristic stories would be an oddity in her mother's long line of failed admirers, though. The young married father of young boys points now with his fork to the book by Lily's plate.

"What do you think?" he asks. His eyes are greenish-gray. His chin glints with stubble.

Lily swallows some pineapple, its acid searing her tongue. "It's fat," she says, trying to recall what she's scrawled in her notebook. "Every sentence is big, flowery. It's a whole world."

Between them, his wife feeds the twins wet chunks of watermelon. "It's the pivot," he says, leaning close. "Interiority. Female agency. Sex. That book broke fiction wide open."

On the cover: Emma Bovary, bored and beautiful. "I feel bad for Charles," Lily says.

"Really?" The writer of futuristic stories looks up from sawing at a dry slab of ham. "I feel worse for Emma. Charles is a blind fool. He only sees what he wants to see."

"I guess," Lily says, sitting up now, forgetting to eat. "But doesn't everyone do that? She married him. Doesn't he have a right to think she loves him?"

"That's the question," the writer says, "isn't it? What does marriage really mean aside from its symbolic power? Charles had choices, but Emma couldn't go to school, get a job."

"Sweetie, please," says the writer's wife, brushing a curd of scrambled egg from her jeans where his fork, flourished for emphasis, has flung it. Lily feels chastened too, sinking back against her chair, embarrassed that his wife had become unreal between them, insubstantial, as the little boys tried their best to digest her, slurping her fingers with their morning fruit.

The writer of futuristic stories dabs at his wife's leg with his napkin. "I get carried away," he says, a blush rising in his cheeks, and Lily feels something rise in her as well, a creeping heat that makes it hard to breathe. Across the table, Lily's mother watches as if she can sense that Lily is suddenly alive from hair root to misshapen baby toenails. Her mother, charismatic wielder of sound and feeling, the woman who once told her, weeping and drunk after a fight with her father, that no one could be blamed for anything done in the service of love, raises her glass of juice as if to make a toast. Lily raises hers as well, sips in solidarity. Then she turns back to the writer of futuristic stories. "My mom says, 'Passion is the artist's fruit.' Wrote it, I mean. In her last book."

He sits back and watches her from that new distance. "That's right," he says. "She did."

Lily picks up her fork. Thrumming, thrumming, thrumming.

After breakfast, Lily is somehow drafted to help install the twins in a black double stroller, the Batmobile of prams. Deanna, the wife of the writer of futuristic stories, thanks her profusely.

"We were here last summer, too," Deanna says, muscled legs brisk behind the wheels as the group of them stroll out into the sun. "Breakfast is fine, but dinners are mystery-meat casseroles. I'm a vegetarian, so I lost thirteen pounds in two weeks."

The boys in the black contraption gabble a continuous stream of nonsense. "I'm shooting for another dozen this time," Deanna says, peering at Lily through sunglasses.

"No way. You're perfect," Lily says, though Deanna just looks like an adult, someone, like Charles Bovary, who believes there is virtue in duty and forgiveness. Her teenage self is almost visible in her thirty-something body, like Venus de Milo returned to her marble block.

"Here we are," Deanna says, stopping by a cottage across the campus from Lily's.

After shaking hands with the playwright, the wizened poet, and Lily's mother, the writer of futuristic stories at last comes to his wife. When he touches the small of her back, Lily sees something in the woman's shoulders visibly let go, her grip loosening on the stroller's handle.

The writer snags the book tucked under Lily's arm, opening it to her tassled bookmark. "You're at the apricots," he says, and hands it back. "Wonderful. The best is yet to come."

She takes the book, thinks of trees split down the middle with lightning. Power lines severed and fizzing. "I know," she says. "My mother told me about the carriage scene."

While Deanna bends to retrieve a pacifier, the writer rocks slightly forward and back. "I envy you," he says. "Reading it for the first time. Don't skim it, now. Don't you dare."

The Wednesday before the students arrive, Lily and her mother sit in front of a laptop at their kitchen table crossing their fingers until her father's call rings through from his dark flat in Egypt. "It's killingly hot," he says. The food, though, is to die for.

"Dad," Lily says, "do you get the Sox out there?" When she was a kid, they'd taken the T from Brookline, paid for same-day cheap seats, and stuffed themselves on ballpark franks a dozen times a summer. Besides one game with her uncle last year, a miserable, rainy slugfest against the Orioles who'd somehow managed to win, she hasn't seen a live game in years.

"I can get anything I want on the Internet," he says, clearly trying not to yawn.

"Right," Lily says, pushing her chair back from his lagging face. "Anything you want."

"Lil," she hears him say as she's tripping to her tiny bedroom. "You know I don't want to be anywhere but home." Both parents call for her to come back, but she is scrawling into her notebook, over and over, *the story is bigger than I am,* the closest her father ever comes to apologizing every time he leaves to watch another corner of the world crumble to dust.

"Sweet dreams, love," Lily hears her mother say, followed by the sound of a kiss.

In three days the campus will fill with writers emerging, established, and aspiring. A contingent will follow her mother from classroom to meals to readings to wine-soaked receptions Lily cannot attend. Every year a man, or sometimes a woman, follows her mother with particular fervor, begging for scraps, prostrate at her feet. As far as Lily knows, her mother has never strayed, and usually Lily enjoys her would-be lovers' inevitable tail-tucked retreat.

But she doesn't want it to happen to the writer of futuristic stories. He doesn't know that her mother feeds on love like a hummingbird on nectar, dipping her thin beak while the rest of her hovers safely out of reach.

For these few days, while her mother writes, Lily tours the empty buildings, floors cool beneath bare feet. One afternoon she follows the breadcrumb squeals of the tiny twins to a fountain where the writer of futuristic stories splashes with his sons in the chlorinated blue.

Deanna lies on a faded blue towel nearby, but props herself up when Lily sits down. "What would you be doing if you weren't here right now?" the woman asks.

Lily watches the writer play with the boys, wet to the elbows of his blue plaid shirt. "Wondering what my mom was doing here," she says without hesitation. "What about you?"

"We have a walnut-colored Arabian. Ginger," she says. "Thursdays are my day to ride."

Lily blushes. She'd expected her to say laundry, or grocery shopping, to be grateful the writer of futuristic stories had taken her somewhere far away from the treadmill of her life. "I've never ridden a horse," Lily says, digging her fingers down among the grass roots into dirt.

"Neither has he," Deanna says, staring at the writer of futuristic stories, her lips twisted into a half-smile. "People think he's done so much. His books, you know. But he's always in a classroom. That's where we met. He was my workshop TA, and I thought he knew everything."

Too much time goes by before Lily asks, "So does he?"

Deanna pushes herself up to sit with her legs in front of her like a girl. The way Lily is sitting. "Sure, he's very bright," Deanna says, staring at the broad spread of her husband's back.

"I have to meet my mom," Lily says, to free herself from this patch of lawn.

Deanna squints up into the sun to look at Lily who is standing now. "It's nice that you're close. I tortured my mother when I was your age."

"My dad says she's too nice. To strangers and stuff. She needs us to look out for her."

Deanna turns back to her family. "She's lucky, then, that you turned out so sweet."

Besides Deanna and the twins, there are other spouses and kids on campus. The one closest to Lily in age is a boy who bends over textbooks, scribbling into a notebook at the picnic table by his cottage. Lily waves whenever she passes. He is a year younger, give or take.

After leaving Deanna and the writer of futuristic stories, Lily hikes to an overlook, loses the path, panics, finds the trail again, and makes it to dinner on time, wasted fear melting sweetly in her gut. The next morning, she walks to the reservoir and finds the textbook boy swimming.

She's learned he's the son of the novelist from Japan and her sculptor husband who smokes a carved wooden pipe in the yard next door. The boy's name is Hiro.

"Mind if I join you?" she asks, a request that seems to her own ears over-formal, a poor man's Audrey Hepburn. He makes no sound. She strips to her suit, walking in until she can float. Hiro swims in silent circles, stealing peeks that redden his cheeks. He's so short and shy that his fourteen years seem like ten. After a few more silent minutes, Hiro leaves her floating.

One day before the students arrive, Lily finds the writer of futuristic stories on the pond's gritty beach when she splashes back onto shore. Hiro has already come and gone.

"I thought you fell asleep out there," says the writer as Lily stands over him, dripping, arms folded under breasts in their pink triangles of fabric, blocking his sun. Her mother bought his new book from the campus store, and Lily had turned to his author page last night. "Think of it, just over twice your age," Lily's mother had said, voice brimming with wonder.

"I'm used to the ocean," Lily says. "There's no waves here. No horizon. It's weird."

He shakes out her towel before stepping close to drape it over her shoulders. Fingers there then gone. Smelling of shaving cream, bug spray, sweat. This is being *alone with someone,* she thinks, a beautiful paradox. She imagines the classroom where Deanna sat, gaze uptilted, one face among many. As if without her permission, Lily's own chin lifts slightly, an offering, but he seems to wake and steps back, half turning away while she secures the towel.

Now he recites from her mother's second book, published the year after Lily was born: "Against her starred palm / ocean pales / as if her wish has willed it."

"I read your book too," she says, though she's only skimmed the first page of every story. Kids clone themselves for fun. Machine guns gain sentience. In the last one, a fissure opens in the earth and someone erects a Club Med over it.

"Don't tell me what you think," he says. "I never read my reviews."

She'd planned to say her mother thought it was "smart and funny, but empty in some essential way," then say she'd missed the point. Lily says nothing instead. She would like to ask him question after question. Why pluck Deanna from the class's ranks? Are they together now for the twins? How can he be so wrong—too old, too taken, too taken with her mother—and still bring to her mouth a cranberry tautness, a readiness to make all kinds of mistakes?

They walk through low brush to the path that leads in one direction back to campus and deeper up the mountainside in the other. *I'm right here,* she thinks at him. *We're both right here.*

"I didn't mean to stop," he says. "Hiro said he saw you. I have something for your mom."

Lily tightens her towel, throat tight. Of course, of course. "I can pass it on," she says.

"Here. It's just a thumb drive. Some music. Did you know she's never heard Bon Iver?"

Lily shakes her head, queasy from the odor of pond water drying on her skin. All the way back to the cottage, her mother's lines ring in her head. "It's natural to want / to be wanted." From her first book, *Myth of Eve,* the one about the affair her father had just before Lily was born. Because it won a major award, it's the one her mother's admirers know best, and treasure.

Saturday the students arrive, filling mountain air with the chirping of automatic locks. Lucky devotees who snag chairs at her mother's table during the first full-company dinner beam at Lily. "Such

9

a pleasure to finally meet you," they say, because they have seen her chalky fetus-shape in "My Dear Hitchhiker," and watched her chip her tooth in "Porcelain." They held her hand on the first day of school, "mossy as something decayed."

Across the room, the writer of futuristic stories is similarly besieged, leaving Deanna alone in this crowd too. Another paradox. Juggling the boys, Deanna catches her eye and winks.

That first night of the real conference, just after her mother leaves for the post-reading reception, a knock sounds on Lily's door. She opens it, heart a jackrabbit, to find Hiro Tanaka shifting foot to foot on her porch. "Our TV died. Can I watch something with you?" he asks.

"I'm watching *Downton Abbey*," she says. "Do you mind?" It's a rerun to boot.

He shrugs.

She steps aside so he can slide past her, then they take up opposite ends of the couch.

"Sybil's my favorite," she says, as Branson tells the youngest Crawley she must choose between everything she knows and all she thinks she wants. Lily has been eating from a bag of Smartfood, and every now and then she holds it out to Hiro so he can take a handful. When the show ends, neither of them wants to watch Charlie Rose, so Lily turns off the TV.

"I think the house came with Connect Four, if you want to play," she says, mostly to fill the silence, but it's touching to see the way his whole face turns to smile when he says "sure." She takes the blue disks while Hiro takes red. Toward the end of their third game, footsteps and laughter sound on the porch. "Connect four!" he says as she goes to peer out the window.

"Isn't this sweet," Hiro's mother says, following Lily's mother into the cottage and letting her hands settle on her son's thin shoulders. Behind the women Hiro's father enters, then the writer of futuristic stories and Deanna, clutching a walkie-talkie—no, a baby monitor receiver—bleary as if she'd just been snatched from sleep.

"Let's say goodnight, Hiro," says the boy's mother, and Lily ducks beneath the woman's beaming gaze, following Hiro out onto the porch, away from the sudden cacophony inside. When he reaches for her, she wonders if he is braver than she thought, but instead of pulling her close, he shakes her hand, firmly.

"Goodnight," she says, flinching from the moth courting her porch light.

She lowers herself to the top step, watching Hiro melt into the night until the screen door squeaks itself open and the writer of futuristic stories settles into one of the creaky rockers.

She can't help but turn to him, sitting almost at his feet as he bends into an orange flame to light a smoke. Maybe he's like all the others, helpless before her mother's radiance, but as her mother herself might say, "Two-faced Janus is the one true god; / change his truest doctrine."

"Boring reception?" she asks. Inside, she hears laughter, the snapping of shuffled cards.

"No worse than usual." He jerks his chin toward Hiro's cabin. "You two have fun?"

Inside, Lily's mother is pouring from a new bottle of wine. Lily thinks of a phrase for her notebook: "I have been the architect of my own night." She studies the stars like spilled sugar.

"Hiro's a nice kid," she says, despite the meager year between them.

"That's not so common," the writer says, dropping his foot to the floor to lean close. "Most grown men—well, you won't find many nice ones."

Close enough to wreath her in his whiskey-musk, he leans even closer to grind his cigarette into a saucer by her wrist, and then—quickly, like the only part of a dream she'll remember on waking—slides his hand up her neck to grip her jaw, not entirely gently. He says her name quietly, that double-flick of the tongue. Then, just as quickly, he's back to rocking, hands in his lap, and she is counting the breaths, twenty-two, before her mother spills onto the porch, swaying toward them in the semi-dark. "M&M poker," her mother says, drunk but not sloppy, working her necklace like a rosary. "Are you two in?"

Inside, Deanna waves with the hand not holding her wine, laughing as if young girls sat on darkened porches with her husband daily. Except, Lily thinks, maybe they do. Maybe Lily is like one of her mother's admirers falling and falling with nowhere to land.

"Next time, for sure," Lily says, retreating to her bedroom, her notebook, her heady dreams.

In the morning, Hiro knocks again. Lily sets down Emma Bovary's terrible, convulsive decline as his hands dance impatiently on the railing. "I found something," he says. Her mother is reading manuscripts. Lily calls through the screen to say she'll see her at dinner.

Hiro is short and slight, but tireless. He leads her past the reservoir, higher up the mountainside than she has been, showing no signs of stopping even when she lags behind, even when pricker bushes ladder their legs with scratches, even when she loses sight of his thrashing progress. She is parched when she finally spots him bending over a bush with green, almond-shaped leaves, pinching light blue berries into his upturned hat.

"Are they safe?" she asks between long sips of air.

"Here," he says, handing her a silver bottle of water, warm but wonderful, which runs in rivulets down her neck. He wipes the rim with his sleeve before drinking. It's hard to believe she was like him once. A serious kid taken up by serious tasks. She doesn't know when things changed, but it was nothing she asked for. If she could go back to the place where Hiro lives, smack between magic and possibility, she'd waste no time.

"How did you find this place?" she asks. The clearing is far from the established path.

"Exploring," he says, and Lily has to bite her cheek at his

matter-of-fact tone. Exploring, for no reason besides the joy of discovery. Of course. When did she quit exploring just for fun?

After they've rested, he shows her the berry's star-shaped bottom and the ripe ones' distinctive bluish-gray, picking them by cupping a bunch and rubbing until ready ones fall and the unripe cling. She likes the hint of his parents' accent neatly clipping the edges of his words. They rinse half a dozen in his warm water and their sweetness on her tongue is startling.

He produces two sandwich bags from a pocket and fills one for her. She tumbles the berries around in their plastic, taut skins rolling like marbles between her fingers. The woods are kinder on the way back, full of sun and shadow. It's not until they are back on campus, pausing to scan the dinner crowd, that Hiro stands on tiptoe to kiss her quickly.

"I like you," he says through purple lips.

She realizes that Hiro has secured a place for himself in her story. Her first kiss, quick as it was. The first feeling, fleeting, is anger. She'd been saving it. Denying others, patient, waiting. Then comes a squirming sort of pity. "Hiro . . ." she begins, but he lifts a hand to point at her mother running awkwardly across the midday lawn, long skirt whipping behind.

"Mama?" she whispers, leaving him.

"Where have you been?" her mother asks, breathless. "It's on the news." Then Lily knows to run with her back to the cottage, air sawing at her throat, where they listen to the BBC describe a massacre at the Republican Guard Barracks in Cairo during dawn prayers. A Welsh journalist on-site claims the military fired on the crowd. "Snipers," her mother says, twisting a thin paper towel around one finger. "God damn your father."

"He's in Alexandria," Lily says. "He's not in Cairo, Mom." But in all likelihood, he ran toward the danger, not away. In all likelihood, he was in the crowd. In all likelihood, her mother has kissed the writer of futuristic stories, at least that, and even if Lily did, now he wouldn't be her first. In all likelihood, her father will call two days from now, tired and gaunt but safe and alive, right on schedule. Her mother Skypes him now, but it just rings and rings and rings.

On Wednesday, Lily and her mother sit on the porch, laptop humming nearby. Lily appeals to logic. Either her father will call, or he won't. Either he will survive this to keep chasing war and pestilence across the globe, or he will—what, give it up to cover dog shows and Pee Wee football? Either her parents will run out of ways to punish each other for sins real and imagined, or they'll be endlessly inventive because it's all they know.

When Hiro wanders over, Lily asks him to tell her everything he knows about plants. He does this, filling the yawning silence, because he still likes her, even after she told him yesterday that she needed him to stay a friend. It was hard to say, but necessary. Kinder than pretending.

"The urushiol in poison ivy oil lasts years on gardening gloves," Hiro says.

Lily watches the screensaver hollow into a funnel, then surge into a mountain, then twist into a slinky, silvery tornado, reversing its fortunes again and again.

Hiro says, "Bamboo grows really fast. Sometimes a meter a day."

Lily's mother drops her head into her hands. It is ten minutes past the usual time.

"Strawberries are the only fruit," Hiro says, "that bear seeds on the outside."

When at last the Skype rings through, the background is light instead of dark. The window is uncurtained, Lily's father is dressed in white. A hospital johnny.

"Oh God," Lily's mother says. Hiro clings to the banister, sinking into silence.

"Everything's fine," Lily's father says. His head has been shaved beneath the bandage. "It just grazed me. I was the luckiest guy in the crowd."

"Come home," her mother says, an expert at speaking through tears. "Now, now, now."

"I fly out tomorrow. But, honey, it was worth it. Just wait until you see my piece."

Their last night in the mountains, Lily accompanies her mother—manic as she's been since the call, relieved, enraged, violently in love—to the final evening reading. Tonight the writer of futuristic stories reads of a city where everyone's lives depend on lines unspooling before them like the London Underground. When people are sick, lines lead them to the doctor. Cancers are caught early. Anxiety is a thing of the past. But when the mapmaker dies without an heir, some people are hit by buses or starve ten feet from cupboards full of food. Some become guides, leading terrified citizens through the rest of their tangled lives. Some retrace the lines they've left behind, reliving the past. The rest flee in droves, drunk on adventure, and die by the dozens, mad with a freedom they'd never known to seek.

After the reading, Deanna asks for Lily's help with the boys. "I would, but—" Lily says, nodding to her mother in conversation a few feet away, just getting to her father's thirty-seven stitches.

"Go, help," Lily's mother says, overhearing, turning back to her rapt listeners. "It's like she's the mother sometimes."

So Lily carries Donnie while Deanna takes Liam, depositing the boys in a Graco crib. At the door, Deanna gathers her lovely hair and pins it up with a blue Bic. "Stay? I have wine."

"I'm pretty tired," Lily says, though the opposite is true. She is too alive to stay.

"Okay, then. Thanks for your help," Deanna says, closing the door but not before Lily sees her face unpin itself and sag away from her bones. Shouldn't she have known, sitting in her husband's long-ago classroom, that others would fall for him too? Isn't it unfair to make all of this Lily's fault? Still, Lily almost falters, almost stays safely away. She almost does, but doesn't.

The receptions are held in a grand white house with a wraparound porch ringed by green hedges. Peeking around an oak's thick trunk, Lily spots her mother through a living room window, students swarming her like fruit flies. Gesturing, her mother's hand glints with rings.

The writer of futuristic stories sits on the porch, chair tipped against the outer wall. When he looks her way, she steps into his line of vision, then rounds the corner of the house and flattens her back against the shingles. As she hoped, he follows.

"Is Dee okay? The boys? Your father?" he says, scotch adhering to his drawl.

"Everyone's fine," she says, wishing she could bat Deanna's name from the air.

"Your mother's inside. I'll grab her—"

"No, don't," she says, reaching out, catching his wrist. "It's just, time's almost up. I just thought—" She doesn't need much. Just to know she's not imagining all of it. And maybe her second kiss. She's young, there are complications, but if he has wanted her, that's something. "I just wanted to see—"

"For yourself," the writer says, shedding her hand to muss his own hair. "I get it. Kids always know more than we think. Well, I'm sorry about all of it now, of course, what with your dad. Not my place, maybe, but don't be too hard on her. If it's anyone's fault, it's mine. She's a beautiful woman, brilliant, and—"

Numbness is setting in from the ankles up when she interrupts, forgets about being kind. "Please, stop. I shouldn't have come," she says, recalling the sweaty heft of his son on her shoulder and the cottage where his wife waits and waits and will keep waiting, his wife who Lily knows now must have seen this a hundred times before, this familiar trap, the dizzy fall. Could it be that Deanna's sadness was for Lily, not herself? She almost feels like laughing. Who better than the wife of the writer of futuristic stories to see how this would play out?

"Oh, now I see." The writer leans against the wall, his shoulder pressing hers. He looks up where a pair of lights reveal a cloud of gnats like summer snow. "I'm writing about you and the Tanaka boy," he says, "only he's called Hugo in the story. You're scientists in an active volcano, field-testing high-heat wetsuits. I'll send it to you when it's done."

Lily swallows against the bitter film coating her tongue. "A volcano," she says.

The writer reaches for her at last, blindly, one hand against her back, drawing her roughly against him, whispering heat into her ear. "You know, that kid's going to spend his whole cursed life looking for another girl like you. You never forget the first one to break your heart."

"It's not what you think," she says, remembering the wasted kiss. She wishes it never happened so she could deny everything the writer thinks he knows about the future.

He releases her and she stumbles back, watching him return to the party and her mother, who will still be the most beautiful woman in any given room for a long time to come. Lily watches him go, then walks home through the dark woods, inventing punishments for writers who believe in clichés as tired as broken hearts.

Desire Comes Closer

It was July, the kind of hot that made me want to lie under the fan in my bedroom, naked to my polka-dotted underwear. Instead my mother, swooping in like the world's best butterfly catcher, trapped my sweaty fingers in long-sleeved rubber gloves and sent me off to the bathroom with the promise of a surprise after everything was scrubbed to a shine.

"The shower curtains have to shine?" I called after her. "The toilet paper?"

"Quit wise-assing, Heather," she called back, and I tried, not because I'd run out of things to say—was the bathmat supposed to shine, the Ivory soap, the rusty razor from the last time Dad came over drunk?—but because she was having a Hard Time and Evil Granny had asked me to go easy on her. I was trying, boy was I trying. So far nothing in my life had been harder.

While I swished the pink toilet brush around the bowl, I tried to work out the surprise. Probably it was a play on dinner. Tuna Surprise, in which the surprise was a topping of crumbled potato chips. But maybe it was a beach day at Alligator Point. Or ice cream, Winn Dixie–brand cookie dough with a squirt of Hershey's. She had me on a diet and didn't know I'd been using birthday money to get Rocket Pops from the truck that roved the park after she left for work.

"You done yet?" she asked after I'd been at it a while, filling up the doorway with the hips she claims made her famous as a girl. "The surprise is here."

"Then I guess I'm done," I said, and peeled off the gloves. The room smelled sharp and bright, like an electric lemon. "Is it ice cream?"

Mama snicked her tongue against the roof of her mouth. "No, Little Debbie. It's not any kind of food."

The doorbell rang then, if you could call it that. The thing just gave a little wheeze like a deflating balloon. I followed Mama to the door, smelling my pruney fingers—lavender soap over that chemical citrus, and a whiff of rubber. I saw two people-shadows on the other side of the door's glass panel. A tall, pudgy one and a short one with pipe-cleaner arms, so it couldn't be Daddy, not that Mama would have thought him much of a reward.

"Susan," a man's voice said when Mama got the door open. "I can't thank you enough."

"Nonsense," she said, and stepped back. The surprise was Cousin Ginger from Atlanta dragging a pink suitcase and looking around like our shag carpet might rear up and bite her.

"Say hello, Heather," my mother said.

"Hello, Heather," I said, and got the slap I probably deserved.

Ginger didn't say much at dinner, just smiled into her lap at her toothpick legs in blue jeans so dark they were almost black. Her shirt was silky, and she wore a long silver necklace that tinkled when she switched the cross in her legs. She was just fourteen, but she looked like an adult and made me feel eight instead of twelve.

"Rosie's at home now, which is good, and bad, for her and us," Uncle Mark was saying, his gaze flicking between Ginger and Mama like he wished there was another language they could talk in. I listened harder. Mama never told me anything about anything, especially bad news. Like with Logan's deployment. We had a party I thought was for my birthday until Mama pulled out his camouflage cake and started bawling. In the last seven months we'd gotten two Skype calls and a postcard with a picture of a camel spider that Mama pinned to the fridge.

Now her sister was dying, Mark's wife, Aunt Rosie of the black, black hair. I'd had clues before, but Uncle Mark confirmed it at dinner. IVs this, chemo that, a wig of curly red hair. I kept sneaking peeks at Ginger while he talked, but she barely seemed to breathe, never mind cry.

"I really can't thank you enough," Uncle Mark was saying, reaching for Mama across the pan of Beef & Macaroni. "A few weeks of quiet and she could turn the corner."

Mama glanced at me, gauging how much I'd caught. "Ginger's always welcome, Mark. Heather needs a playmate anyway. She's spent the whole summer with her nose in a book."

"Not just one book," I said. I'd read sixteen so far. "Besides, all my friends went on vacation." It came out whiny, like I was begging to go to Cancún, and I felt bad. Mama had told me often enough how expensive I was on top of the rest: electricity, food, gas. "If Gus paid an inkling of what he owes," she'd say, and end up shaking her head. Logan sent checks, but Mama pinned them to the fridge too. She said we weren't that bad off yet.

"More green beans?" Mama asked Ginger. My cousin shook her head no, smiling with her mouth closed. Uncle Mark watched her, forehead lined like the sheet music for my recorder.

"What kind of cancer is it?" I asked. Mama grabbed my wrist tight enough to milk it for venom, but I didn't back down. Soon Uncle Mark would leave, and I had no guarantee Ginger would fill in the blanks. It seemed she'd forgotten the rudiments of the English language.

Uncle Mark set down his fork. "Heather, it's in her uterus. Do you know what that is?"

Ginger threw her head back to let out a shrieking laugh. "Gee, Dad, what's a uterus?" she screeched before slumping back against her chair, more giggles trickling out of her. My mother gripped the table edge, eyes wild, but Ginger seemed tired after that, spent, and grew quiet again.

While I was washing the dishes, I got another tidbit. If I turned down the water, I could hear Mama and Mark out by his car, indistinctly. "Ginger's upset, naturally," Uncle Mark was saying, "but her behavior—*something*. Rosie's just worn out, and I *something, something, something*. Really, we can't thank you enough."

"Sometimes it's easier to be angry than sad," Mama said, and whatever Uncle Mark said to that I couldn't hear.

Later that night, much later, Ginger whispered my name. I sat up like I was waiting for my cue. "You want to get out of here?" she asked. I nodded, remembered it was too dark to see, then whispered to let me get on my jeans.

In my mother's room, the TV draped its blue curtain over the sleeping hill of her while a standing fan muffled her snores.

We went out the front because the back steps were squeaky. The other trailers were dark and buttoned up, all except for the Lawrence sisters, whose game shows lit their living room all night long. The white dirt roads we walked were silvered over, liquid looking, and Mrs. Brawn's daylilies by the entrance had closed up like duck beaks. We headed for the main road and the 24-hour 7-Eleven. Ginger wanted smokes.

"My mom has a carton," I said, hooking my thumb toward home, but Ginger didn't slow. She was wearing the same jeans she'd arrived in, but had changed into a black tank top that left an inch of creamy skin uncovered on her stomach.

"Getting them is half the fun, cuz," she said, and shook out her hair, dragging a cherry Chapstick across her lips. We were the only ones on the sidewalk, the main road empty except for the occasional low-riding Buick or dented pickup that didn't slow. I felt underdressed in a black T-shirt, one of my favorites, that read "Have Your Tribble Spayed or Neutered."

There was a little crowd out in front of the store, guys in

wifebeaters sitting on the hoods of their broad-hooded cars, and a few girls moving to the beat of the Top 40 hits pouring through the windows, hair pulled back in ponytails so tight their eyes were drawn long and the skin around them lineless. I hung back, seeing them, and Ginger slowed too, but not in the same way. She put a hitch in her step, whipped her hips side to side with each forward strut, and stared straight ahead with no trace of a smile, letting no gaze latch onto hers.

I scuttled to keep up. "Maybe we should go home," I said, feeling more like a child than ever, wanting the stillness of the kitchen, the rickety stepstool beneath me as I felt around in the freezer for the half-gone carton of my mother's "Marble Lites."

"This will just take a minute," Ginger said, and stopped to glance at me so I could see her sharp sliver of a smile. I'd thought after we got ready for bed that she might talk about her mother or whatever happened in Georgia that got her sent here, but she'd just burrowed into her sleeping bag. Even in her stillness a kind of life had emanated from her, a pulse that kept me rigid and awake until her whisper.

She didn't seem the same girl who'd massacred me at Monopoly while everyone snoozed last Thanksgiving, knocked out by the pair of Peking ducks Evil Granny bought with her China Delite employee discount. When Ginger won, I called her lucky, but she'd just waved her candy-colored bills. "People make their own luck," she'd said. "Quicker you learn that, the better."

Now she wore perfume smelling of sugar cookies, and it spilled over me when she bent to look me in the eye. "I can't do this without you, cuz. Nothing bad will happen, I promise." Her teeth gleamed white beneath the buzzing streetlight.

I tried to smile, but it wouldn't come, so I nodded instead.

"Hey girl," the calls started as soon as we left our curb and the boys grabbed their belt buckles, rubbed at the sandpaper on their jaws. The girls crossed their arms under considerable chests, sucked at cigarettes, and turned their backs as if we didn't exist.

Ginger walked into their midst, the sea of bodies parting for her until one guy, tall, shaggy-haired, face yellowed by the streetlight, a delicate silver chain around his neck with the charm a discreet mystery under his white T-shirt, stepped out in front of her, where he shifted gently side to side like a man on a boat.

"Excuse me," she said firmly, flicking her eyes to his.

He stood with his lower body thrust gently forward. "Oh shit, am I in your way, doll?"

She leaned back on a heel. "That's what 'excuse me' generally means."

"Forgive me, your highness," he said, showing us callused palms crisscrossed with lines that sometimes intersected and sometimes didn't.

Ginger passed him and I followed. The boys high-pitched the calls of night birds after us until one of the girls leaned into a car window and turned the music way, way up. "Maybe we shouldn't—" I said, but Ginger just reached into her pocket and pulled out some change.

"Get a Snickers or something, and count it out slowly. Only use half of your giant brain."

I let the warm coins fill my hands. Inside, the candy display vibrated with fluorescent light, and I stood before it in the chilled air like I was weighing M&Ms over Kit-Kats, Starbursts over Twix. The young clerk was skinny with lank orange hair and a constellation of zits in front of his right ear. He nodded to me, then his gaze flicked to Ginger and stayed there. She smiled big as she flirted with the counter, brushing against a can of Slim Jims, reaching into a plastic bin of lighters, flicking one into orange flame, then dropping it back in the bin. Set back on the counter was a rack of Parliaments, menthols, with a handwritten sale price of $5.99.

"What do you think, cuz?" she asked brightly, hands on knees like I was six or seven, having a hard time picking out my treat. Then, to the clerk, "Chubs here is a candy freak."

I was too shocked to do more than shrug. I knew we were

just pretending, but it still stung. Chubs. It was true that I was bigger than most girls my age, but I'd only ever felt that way after something reminded me, like seeing my reflection in a group, or snagging on my frozen face in one of pictures Mama preserved between the plastic leaves of our family albums. I hated Ginger in that moment for seeing me that way almost as much as for dragging me into her plot.

And yet, at the same time, it was thrilling to be out in the world at night, on a level with those kids in the parking lot who were the undeniable epitome of cool. It was exciting to think of Mama snoozing in front of an infomercial for a chicken rotisserie while we bamboozled this clerk, who I recognized now as Derek Oulette, the older brother of a boy in my grade, while Ginger seduced him. I set down a bag of Skittles and picked up an Almond Joy.

Ginger ruffled my sleep-mussed hair and looked at Derek like *isn't she precious*, then leaned over me again, sort of bouncing her boobs around in her shirt.

"Me, I'm a fool for Reese's Pieces," she said. I could smell her perfume again, warm vanilla, and the clerk's cinnamon gum, and I slapped the bag of Reese's down, spilling my handful of change onto the Plexiglas, obscuring the lottery tickets trapped below. At the same time, Ginger bumped into the Slim Jims, scattering them so some fetched up against the register and some plunged over his side of the counter.

"Oops," she said, going up on tiptoe and stretching her shirt at the same time so the neckline plunged. Derek's face went red, and he sunk out of sight to collect the spilled tubes of meat. That's when Ginger took a pack of cigarettes and tucked it in my back pocket, where the corners dug into my butt.

I must have made some sound, a squeak, because Ginger squeezed my shoulder, nails taking root. "How much is this?" she called, shaking the Reese's, and Derek rose with bouquets of Slim Jims clutched in each fist.

"One dollar and seven cents," he said, tripping over the final sibilant *s*, and I finished counting it out, slowly, as Ginger had instructed.

He gathered the dimes and nickels and pennies. "Night," he said in a deflated voice, as if he knew he'd been had. He would count the cigarettes after we left and know for sure, and then I would have to avoid his eyes the next time I came in. My stomach turned as I followed Ginger outside with our contraband waggling under my long T-shirt like a dog's stub tail.

My cousin led the way through the band of kids Mama would've called riffraff, and threw the Reese's to the tall guy who had stopped us on our way in. He caught them one-handed.

After we'd left the older kids behind, Ginger slung her arm around my shoulders.

"We're a hell of a team, cuz," she said. I handed her the cigarettes, then watched her toss them onto the railroad tracks below the little bridge we were crossing. "I don't smoke," she said.

Evil Granny came by in the morning lugging a garbage bag full of fortune cookies. "Jie had to get rid of these," she said, setting her burden on the kitchen pass-through. A scarf covering her perm was knotted under her chin. "Come here, Ginger Marie. Give Granny a hug."

Ginger shuffled over in her shorts cut so high the pockets hung out in front and back. While Evil Granny enfolded her in praying mantis arms, outside Mama fussed with her flower barrels, singing a hymn in a wavery voice. "Fight the Good Fight," I thought it was. Up close, I knew Evil Granny smelled of stale smoke and chow mein. She wasn't a big hugger, but I got one after my dad left, and if anybody needed one now, it was Ginger. Still, it burned, watching them.

All day, while Ginger and I drained a bottle of grape juice and flipped around between Saturday morning cartoons, sweating into the velveteen couch, I'd waited for her to talk about her mother, or what we pulled last night. When she said nothing, I'd pointed to a commercial for Skittles and said we should go after a bag of those next. She'd only downed another cup of juice and flipped past some gyrating butts on MTV to an episode of *Adventure Time* I'd already seen.

Now, though, she leaned all her weight into Evil Granny's barstool, shoulders shaking with her face pressed against one of those old, bony shoulders. I was the one who'd sat inside with her all this gorgeous day. I'd risked my hide last night only to have her throw away all the fruits of our labor. It was my shoulder she should have been crying on. Instead I had to listen to Evil Granny croaking in her leathery voice, "I know, Toots. I know, I know, I know."

I switched off the TV and Mama's voice got louder. *"Run the straight race through God's good grace / Lift up thine eyes and see His face,"* and so on through the screen.

"What are we supposed to do with these?" I asked, reaching into the bag and bringing out one crinkly plastic-wrapped package.

"They're expired. No use to the restaurant, thanks to the Federal Department of Assholes. I thought you could sell them by the road. You got a card table, right?"

"Like a lemonade stand?" I asked, my cheeks gathering heat. "We're not babies."

Granny took one hand off Ginger's back to shake a ring-choked finger at me. "You weren't too old for it last year when your mom and dad were in Daytona. You must have sold four gallons of Country Time at a 200 percent profit. And I don't recall you sharing a dime with the sainted lady who made you those three dozen snickerdoodles either."

"Well, that was last year," I said, plucking at my shirt to get some air down there. The $65 I made had bought a dozen Goosebumps books at the Goodwill. And candy too. A ton of it.

Ginger knuckle-dried her eyes. "I don't know," she said. "It could be fun. What about the lot across from the 7-Eleven? You got a wheelbarrow, Heather?"

"A wagon," I said, watching her.

"Granny, can I borrow your scarf?" Ginger asked.

"That's more like it," Evil Granny said, handing it over along with ten dollars for markers and posterboard. A paper tablecloth. Napkins to give out with each sale.

The stand looked like this: card table draped in a red sheet; glass globe liberated from our porch light and filled with smoke from a cigarette Ginger borrowed from Mama's open pack; white sign reading "Fortunes by Madame Mumbo-Jumbo, $2 each"; and a folding chair beneath a rainbow beach umbrella where Ginger sat, Evil Granny's scarf swathing her head like a turban.

I sat under the table with the bag of fortunes, trying to keep sugar ants out of my shorts.

With her hair in pigtails under the turban and a smile framing Chiclet teeth, Ginger looked a decade younger than last night. Every time someone passed, she'd call out, "Fortunes for charity," or "Help me start a college fund," and the person would come over, the young mother with two babies sleeping beneath the beach blanket rigged over their stroller, an old man with his walker cushioned by two gray tennis balls, a pair of high school girls giggling over so many inside jokes their speech was a foreign language.

Each time she got a customer, Ginger put her forehead against the cloudy globe and closed her eyes, asking the universe to guide her in a shivery voice, at the same time reaching under the table for the cookies I'd stripped from their bags, signaling one or two or three. She'd pretend to emerge from her trance, crack open the cookie on the top of the globe, and hand it to the customer saying, "Thank you, come again."

Most customers laughed, read their fortunes out loud, and handed Ginger the money, but a few cried foul. "If I wanted to hear about 'a wind of change,' I'd have checked the weather," said the old guy with the walker, and a lady clicking a cough drop against her teeth said in a gravelly voice, "Got the same damn one at China Delite last week." The legend on Cough Drop's slip was "Face facts with dignity." After she huffed off, Ginger said if she had a mug like hers she wouldn't want to face it with dignity or anything else, and we cracked up.

"Anyway, she's right," I told Ginger. "Evil Granny is their lunchtime hostess," and added that the owner, Jie Wu Sun, was her old, wrinkly boyfriend.

"Why do you call her that?" Ginger asked, puffing on the refry of Mama's cigarette to fill up that globe some more, and stretching her legs under the table so I had to duck.

"Something Daddy said," I started, pulling at the scraggly grass while I figured out how to explain it. He'd come home one Sunday from Lake Overstreet drunk and pissy. Mama told him her mother was coming for dinner, and he'd said, "If I was on fire that woman wouldn't spit to put me out. She's one evil—" At which point Granny pushed in the door with a covered dish.

"Go on, Augustus," Granny went, and he turned red while she laughed. "Hear that, Heather?" she said to me. I was doing long division at the table. She said, "You got stuck with one evil witch for a granny." The next day Daddy split, probably because Granny caught him talking shit after all his blather about being a good man Mama should be grateful for. And even when he showed up now and again, he wasn't so mean, and sometimes he brought steaks or crawdads, and I hadn't seen him smack Mama in months. It was like Granny had fixed him.

"It's kind of like her superhero name, or something," I finished, and it sounded dumb, but by the way Ginger fell into her arms earlier, I figured she'd know just what I meant anyway.

"Huh," Ginger said.

Just *huh*. She didn't get it, and didn't get me, and just like that I was sick of babysitting her. I counted our stash. "We got forty-six bucks," I said. "Let's quit at fifty and get Popsicles."

All I heard was the shush of her knees against the tablecloth as she recrossed her legs.

"Gin?" I called, peering through the red sheet toward the street where I saw the scabbed ankles of the boy from last night in sneakers that may have once been white.

"You again," he said, exaggerating his drawl. "New to the region, Miss Mumbo?"

When her chair squeaked, I knew she was standing, and that if I lifted the cloth that divided us, I'd see she'd taken off her turban and had shifted in those short shorts and tiny top until she looked the way she had last night, sinuous, sexy, strong, and a hell of a lot older than fourteen. The more I heard him talk, the more I thought I recognized him as the cashier in the Shell station, which made him at least eighteen.

"Gin," I said again, but she was haggling. Two fortunes for a dollar, one for each of them. Her hand came under the table, two fingers held out. I grabbed her hand so she had to squat and look me in the eye. "It's almost dinnertime," I said. "Please let's go home."

"There's more to life than food, Heather," she said, smiling with a sad little twist to her lips. "Hand me two fortunes. We have a customer."

I wished for some of Evil Granny's strength, or Superman's laser eyes, but all I did was hand over the cookies, numb and silent. "No one can walk backwards into the future," she read.

"That's some mumbo-jumbo all right," he said, and instead of the crack of his cookie, the next sound I heard was soft, slippery, suctiony, like Evil Granny and Jie when they said goodbye after a shift. I knew if I poked my head out I'd see them mashed against each other, writhing.

"Ginger," I said, loud this time. No one had asked me to look out for her. No one said, "Heather, your cousin's in a rough place and she might do something out of grief and pain that she'll later regret." I guess when it came down to it, no one had to. It was obvious even to me that she was looking for a kind of trouble that announced itself as such instead of working in silence like the cancer intent on erasing her mother from a world where some lucky people could still bitch about work and argue and garden and get high and fight wars and hold hands in blissful denial of the expiration dates inked invisibly on each of our foreheads.

I was gathering my courage to emerge when she crouched down again and lifted the cloth. "Want to take a turn as the swami?" She held out Evil Granny's scarf. "I'll be right back. I have to go help Kenny with something, then we'll go home, okay?"

Her hair was still in pigtails. At close range the sun revealed a smattering of freckles across her nose. She looked even younger than I felt, my hairy legs crusted with sand and grit, arms lumpy and bug-bitten, in a My Little Pony T-shirt. "Okay," I said, and took the scarf, when I should have said, "This is bullshit. Help me pack up this crap and lug it home. Don't go anywhere with that scabby, greasy-haired, burned-out creepazoid."

She gave me a hand up. Kenny didn't seem to see me. His jaw was stippled with a three-day beard, his T-shirt tentlike. She went around the table and his hand buried itself in the right pocket of her skimpy shorts. I saw the meat of her thigh draw up when he squeezed.

"Ginger, wait," I said. Evil Granny's scarf lay limp in my hands, retaining none of her righteous, creep-busting power. My cousin turned just enough to toss a wink, then trotted across the street with that rod-skinny, loose-limbed man, disappearing behind the 7-Eleven.

I waited a long time. Without Ginger's mystique to lure them, no passerby even slowed, and after thirty minutes of failure I emptied the mist from our crystal ball, balled up the table cloth, pocketed the cash, and packed the wagon.

Ginger didn't come and didn't come and didn't come. She had a cell phone, but I didn't, and though I had two quarters for the pay phone across the street, I didn't have her number. Overhead, a cluster of live oaks whispered at the rush of wind that precedes one of our famous afternoon rainstorms. I rearranged the wagon so I could sit in it and set the table up over me like a roof. The storm was brief and left everything dripping and clean-smelling for a few minutes before the mosquitos found me again. The sun sank behind a gray curtain. I took a chance and left the stuff to circle the 7-Eleven, but all I saw behind it was the clerk's rusted Volvo parked crookedly by an overflowing Dumpster and a bunch of soggy cardboard.

I knew it would be just a matter of time before one of the vehicles swishing by on the wet road offered me a ride. I'd already waved past Mr. Delahunt and his son, who lived in the new development, and Old Miss Sally, who had the most desirable trailer of them all to my mind, the one that backed into forest, Spanish moss dripping over her patchy grass, where any kid was welcome to use the ancient tire swing hanging from one of the live oak's way-high branches.

The one who finally insisted I *get my butt in this instant* was Mrs. Riley with the twins in the back seat and a paper sack of groceries up front. We put the wagon and table in the way back. It had started sprinkling again, and I asked her to idle a minute while I checked behind the store one last time. There were no more clues than the first time, but I cupped my hands around my mouth and bellowed into the greenery: "Ginger, come on. It's time to go home."

The only answer was the muted crunch of gravel as a car pulled up out front, and a breeze through the kudzu blanket in the thin woods at the edge of the lot. There were paths through that tangle of green to a cluster of houses. I imagined their warped walls molded and scaled with chipping paint, yards knee-high with thistle. Mrs. Riley was waiting for me, but I thought about going back there anyway, tearing through the jeweled webs of orb weaver spiders, tripping on rotting logs, startling water moccasins that lingered in the drainage ditch separating the parking lot and the neighborhood. Maybe Ginger was just sitting on one of those porches, sipping a beer, perfectly content. Maybe she was splayed out on a stained mattress laid bare to the floor, pinned down by strong arms, murdered, kidnapped, or something even worse.

Wherever she was, I didn't go back there. Mrs. Riley was waiting.

I had an hour to watch reruns before Mama got home from the Olive Garden, oily apron bunched in a fist. When I told her Ginger was gone, I braced for the crack of her hard palm, but Mama didn't do anything except sit on the couch next to me, her pink-striped tie tickling the cup of my ear when I put my head in her lap. While I dozed in front of an old episode of *Cheers*, she called in a Missing Persons Report with Sheriff Greenly, who told her not to worry too much yet. "You know teenagers," I heard him say.

"She better get home before her father gets here," Mama said after they hung up.

"Uncle Mark's coming back already?" I asked, hoping I sounded disappointed. I wasn't, though. I was hoping she'd leave as soon as possible and without a fuss. It was too hard to keep up with her, and today proved there was nothing I could do to keep her safe or cheer her up.

Mama only grunted, and I fell asleep with her stroking my tangled hair until Ginger came in during the late-night news. She was dirt from toes to shoulders. I could smell pond water on her from across the room. It was a different smell from the lake Daddy fished, where he generally hooked half a dozen crappies and blue-gills hardly worth the work of boning.

"I need a shower," Ginger said, crossing her arms over her stomach and then changing her mind, letting them hang down by her sides.

Mama went to her, taking hold of her shoulders. "Your father is on his way," she said. "He called me at work. Said he'd been trying to reach you."

"I got his message." Ginger studied her dirty toes. "So much for my country vacation."

Mama pulled her in for a hug, mud and all, but instead of melting like with Evil Granny, Ginger stayed stiff as a stick of dynamite, hands dangling off her wrists. While she showered, I tried to pump Mama for information, but all she allowed was Aunt Rosie had taken a turn. I would have tried harder, but I remembered all at once that Rose was Mama's sister and Evil Granny's daughter. I felt real small then, and sorry, for giving either of them any extra grief.

Ginger was packed and napping when her father pulled in around two in the morning. "Made you some coffee," Mama said, pouring him some of the bitter-smelling stuff in a mug that he drained without the aid of milk or sugar. I pretended to still be asleep on the couch.

"Can't thank you enough for taking her, Susan," Uncle Mark said. His black slicker was drenched and dripping, rain remnants oozing down his sleeves like oil.

Mama shushed him, then told him how Ginger came home all wet and surly. Uncle Mark set his empty mug carefully on the bar, head hanging like someone had snipped the muscles at the back of his neck. "Last month, I found her in our basement with two boys, pockets full of her mother's painkillers. Before that, the cops brought her home. We thought she was at field hockey practice. That's not the half of it, if you can believe it. We thought, out here, what could happen?"

Mama put a finger to her lips, then told me to check on Ginger. Sitting up, I stared hard at Uncle Mark. If he'd warned me, I'd have tried to keep her home with Scattergories and *The Princess Bride*. He hadn't helped her, pretending nothing was wrong, and did me no favors either. The longer I stared, though, the more his shoulders seemed to slope, the grayer his face seemed. He was a cardboard cutout of a man. I could have torn him in half with one word.

In my room, Ginger lay on the bed. "Your cut's twenty-three dollars," I said.

She sat up but didn't turn around. "Keep it," she said, shoving her arms into a fuzzy white cardigan with pearl buttons. Now she was dressed like a tiny executive in a charcoal gray A-line dress with a zipper up the side, and square-toed high-heeled shoes. Her black hair was wet from the shower, slick and shiny in the overhead light. Only her face gave her away. It was puffy and white, pinchable, pokeable, still just a kid's. "Buy yourself some Skittles."

I reached back to pull the wad of money from my pocket. "You did all the work," I said, pretending she hadn't spoken, or that her words weren't meant to hurt. "You deserve it, really."

"I don't fucking want it," she said, and dug around in her bag until she found another handful of cash, tugging it from the shorts she'd been wearing earlier and tossing it on the bed. The smell of pond water wafted from it. "I don't want this either."

I froze with her half of the money held out. She stood and went out to the living room, with her suitcase following like an obedient dog.

At the front door, Uncle Mark lifted his arm and Ginger went there, snugging into the space beneath his armpit. My father wasn't all bad, of course. He'd showed me how to tie knots he learned in the navy and took me fishing sometimes, but he had never in all my recollections made that simple gesture. There were hugs, but not like that one. Next to Uncle Mark, I saw all Ginger's features finally settle into place and she looked no age but fourteen, mouth drawn but holding steady, eyes dry but wide, as if in disbelief. If I envied Ginger for her flat stomach or her daring, the thing I most wanted was right there in front of me, and I could tell she didn't even know what she had. But I guess that's the way of things. Everyone else's grass, and all that.

"Take care now," Mama said, and ran a hand down Ginger's long fall of damp hair.

When they'd finally left, headlights scissoring through the

rainy night, I counted Ginger's damp money. It came to $220. I gave Mama the whole wad, plus our profit. She counted it, clucking her tongue, then looked out the window the way Ginger had gone.

"Heather, I thank my lucky stars you're mine," she said. "I hope you thank yours, too."

Later, after Aunt Rosie's funeral, after Ginger went away to a place out West for troubled girls, I saw Kenny again, not at the Shell, but behind the counter at the liquor store where Evil Granny was buying sherry for the restaurant. I followed her in to help with the bags and pick out a scratcher, wrinkling my nose at the spoiled grape smell. Each ticket glittered with promises, the Monopolies, the Lucky Red 7s, the Wheel of Fortunes. I was studying them when he spoke.

"Mumbo-Jumbo's friend," Kenny said. "Isn't that right?"

I looked around for Evil Granny, but she was off in the bowels of the store, haranguing a worker into getting some dusty bottles off a top shelf.

"Cousin," I said stiffly. "Her name's Ginger."

Kenny looked less scruffy than I remembered. His hair was combed. He'd shaved. "She took the cash in my wallet while I was in the can," he said, shoving two fingers into each pocket like a gunslinger. "Crazy girl went and jumped in that puddle by the water treatment plant, too. Dove in clothes and all. I told her she'd catch some bad shit in there, but she just laughed."

"She's in Idaho now. Her mom died," I said. I didn't know why I was telling him the truth, why I was talking to him at all. I had let it happen, whatever he did to Ginger in one of those houses behind the 7-Eleven. Even if she'd wanted it, he'd been no help to her.

But now he was nodding. "Her mom, that's right," he said. "Tough break. Tell her I said what's up if you see her. Tell her there's no hard feelings."

"Give me a Treasure Hunt, please. My granny'll pay." I

pointed to the ticket beneath the Plexiglas, and he reached down to tear one from the roll.

"She told my fortune," he said, sliding me the square. "Gave me this cookie that said 'Change begins with you.' After she cleaned me out, I wanted to kill her. I'd been saving for—" He shook his head and crossed his arms tight over his shirt. "Shit. Anyway, I never bought any since. She was crazy, but she did me a kind of favor. Why don't you tell her that, too."

Granny was finally coming with a silver-haired man carrying a pot belly before him like a great bass drum and three sherry bottles in each arm.

"Sure," I told Kenny, one notch in Ginger's belt who'd given her more than the contents of his wallet. "Will do." But I never did tell her anything he said.

And years later, I left my own good luck out of letters addressed to her in rehab or jail. I'd kept all the cookies that Evil Granny gave us, each growing crumblier with the passing years, and I glued in the strips they housed instead of news about college or jobs. Just the good ones, though. "You will achieve a lifelong goal," and "The object of your desire comes closer," and "Success is a journey, not a destination." I only sent ones that looked forward, because what's done is done is done.

That's what I was thinking in the liquor store. Even if Kenny took himself to Atlanta one day and saw a kid spotting flies in a Little League game with a forehead broad like his, the same weak chin and not-quite-wavy hair, even if I told him everything, what could it bring but regret?

Evil Granny gave me a nickel before starting up the car. "Give it a whirl," she said.

The scratcher was a winner, $3. Just enough to buy another one. When Granny asked, though, I said it was a dud, and never cashed it. That's another thing I've kept all these years.

Firebug

It starts as a buildup of energy rising from curled toe-tips up your legs to fill the space behind your eyes. As always, you think you can control it, but in the next second your sister's hair is burning, split ends giving off a familiar smell of crisping coconut shampoo.

Everyone is used to your fits, and Margaret doesn't even scream. Instead she grabs one of the damp washcloths your family keeps around the house and tears open its Ziploc casing. The little packages are everywhere—flung over staircase banisters, balancing on doorknobs, wadded up on the ancient, bulky television. It's your chore to wash these cloths often. Most have scorch marks burned into their soft, no-color fibers. Considering your condition, it's a small miracle there's only been one major fire, when you were just a baby. This time, your sister extinguishes her hair, then dials her stylist while tendrils of smoke rise from her head in sinuous threads. She gets a special rate for emergency trims. A frequent-customer thing.

While she waits for Mad Cutters to pick up, Margaret glares at you from across the room. You should be practicing Ujjayi breath, but instead you glare back, holding your ground for once, shaky though it may be. A week ago, you would not have had this argument, but a week ago the boy in Driver's Ed hadn't asked if you were going to the Junior Ring Dance, which Margaret is in charge of organizing.

You've never been to a dance, or wanted to go, but no one cared if you went before, especially no one like the boy with his array of brightly colored Sharpies who pens portraits on your hands in the back of Mr. Baum's modified Civic while the other student driver jerks you around your small town.

He'd asked if you were going to the dance, which is not the same as asking you to go with him. Still, you want to see him outside of Mr. Baum's backseat, even if it might be dangerous. You told him you were going with friends, which was risky, since you have none. He nodded, adding blue feathers to the parrot he'd outlined on the back of your right hand, the felt tip of his pen raising pins and needles in the soles of your sandaled feet. When Mr. Baum dropped you at home, you asked Margaret if you could ride to the dance with her. She laughed before realizing you were serious, then put a hand on your arm.

Jessie, she said, what if someone pisses you off and you pull a *Carrie*?

I haven't had an incident since January, you said, and that's five months ago. At least, you added silently, no major ones. Even then, only the mailbox was hurt, with its burden of slick college brochures reminding you how Margaret would go into the world soon and you would watch her leave from your bedroom window like a cloistered Victorian madwoman. These days Margaret brings the mail in from its new flame-retardant box.

No, she'd said, squeezing gently, I don't think the dance is a good idea.

That was all it took to ignite a burst. You fought it all the way, and were lucky it was a small one, but Margaret's smoldering hair ended up proving her point.

I'm going, you say now, getting your breath back. Whether you like it or not.

She turns away, speaking to her hairdresser, whose thick Eastern European accent leaks through the cell.

It's easy for Margaret to say no when she's been to every

dance and game and pep rally you have sat out. In the past, you did it gladly. Smugly. You were above it. But now it seems unfair. And you are better at controlling your condition now. Only the tips of her hair were damaged. It's a definite improvement.

If Margaret had been born with pyrokinesis like you, maybe she'd understand what it meant to have Sharpie Boy look through the fringe of his bangs and say he was going to stop by the dance with his buddies. But she was born perfect, and stayed that way.

This is not to say Margaret is wrong about the dance. The onset gives you little warning. When it rushes up from the soles of your feet, you feel that if you don't project it out and away, your body will spontaneously combust. Which is impossible, according to Mr. Geldon, your chem teacher. But then, so is your disease.

You've managed not to be a freak at school by keeping to the back rows, striving for middle-of-the-road grades that don't get you noticed. You have no close friends, on purpose. Your family protects you, and you try not to burn them up. Going to the dance would be reckless, but you are tired of playing it safe.

Your mom's theory is hormones. You'll outgrow it like you outgrew the Backbeat Boys. It's Backstreet, you've told her again and again. And though no amount of torture, blackmail, or bribery could drag it out, you still have a thing for Nick Carter.

You're right, as usual, you tell Margaret, when she hangs up, though when she leans in for a hug, you pretend to tie your shoe, and keep your real decision to yourself.

Your house is bordered on three sides by water. Whether this is by design, as you suspect, or coincidence, as your parents swear— they've lived on the Cape since long before you were born—it does seem convenient since, as a child, your fits could be quelled by tossing you in the ocean just before the fireworks began.

You think it was the distraction more than the water that stopped you, but your parents only knew it worked. Until it stopped working when puberty hit. In elementary school your fits came twice a year, sometimes three, but in junior high they started coming every other week. The uptick scared you, especially since your parents quit looking for a cure. Even when they could get a doctor to believe, no one knew how to treat you. So now your mother says, Hormones, like a mantra, and tracks your calm streaks on the calendar.

You are sixteen and a half—old enough to apply for your Massachusetts junior operator's license, provided you pass Driver's Ed. You are two supervised sessions from done, but driving scares the crap out of you. It's not the mechanics you fear, but the ticking time bomb of your temper during traffic standstills.

Your Driver's Ed teacher, Mr. Baum, knows about your condition. The other drivers are Tanya the Goth Girl and Sharpie Boy, who you've liked since he transferred from St. Sebastian's. While Mr. Baum zip-zip-zips at Tanya to enter the rotary, the boy draws on you in the backseat until you have to practice *pranayama*, yogic breath control that sometimes delays your fits, which arise from any excess of emotion, good ones included.

Mr. Baum prods the others to engage their blinkers, adjust their mirrors, keep their hands at ten-and-two. During halting three-point turns, he times them. When you drive, he holds a squirt bottle of water as if you are a wayward house pet. So far you have been too distracted while driving to muster the energy for a fit, but you fear the day driving becomes second nature, when a bout of road rage could go terribly, terribly wrong.

I'm so stressed, your sister says at the dinner table. The dance is two weeks away; preparations are reaching critical mass. She's pressed friends into service as ticket takers and decorators. Her boyfriend, Rodney, will man the snack table, but he is not happy about it. He'd rather smoke joints by the track shed with his friends.

Margaret thinks you have given up on the dance, but you are planning to bike there in one of her dresses. She will not want to seem like a bitch in front of her friends and will let you buy a ticket at the door. You stole a pink tube dress from her closet, and a pair of sparkly heels. You have to squash a tiny burst now, shoveling in a mouthful of salad and chewing steadily, at the thought of Sharpie Boy seeing you dressed up. You are afraid of dancing with him, but are more afraid of staying home to watch *Sense and Sensibility*. Again.

Now your mother nods in sympathy with Margaret and takes some salad. You notice with pleasure she's trapped a tomato in the tongs, as well as a few sunflower seeds, which are rich in vitamin E. Your mother eats like a bird, according to your father. You wish she ate like something larger. A cat, or even a wolf. You'd like her to wolf down something besides salad. Her bones seem as hollow as the pipes your father plumbs.

The dance will be great, your mother tells Margaret, shunting her tomato aside. You wish, not for the first time, that you'd developed any other neural disorder than the one you have—telekinesis, so you could move a piece of chicken to her plate; telepathy, so you could plant the suggestion that she eat more.

What about you, Jessica? your father says, mildly, carefully. Better safe than roasted.

What *about* me? you say, spearing a transparent slice of cucumber.

Your parents don't actually demand that you skip activities; they call it the mature choice. You can't wait to shame them with their lack of faith in you.

Jessie's not going, your sister says, listing things that could go up in flames. Crepe paper. Tablecloths. Cheese Doodles. Overly sprayed hair. She is not trying to be cruel, but your annoyance creeps into anger.

You ask to be excused.

When your father agrees, you sprint to the backyard just in time to ignite one candle-sized flame in the petunias. When you stamp it out with the clogs you wear for this purpose, the damage is so negligible that you decide it doesn't count against your streak.

The week before the Junior Ring Dance, Mr. Baum is late picking the three of you up. You wait with Tanya and the boy, who whistles "Eye of the Tiger." After a minute it's clear that Tanya is staring at you. Hard.

You keep looking for Mr. Baum as if you are anxious to hit the open road.

How do you do it? Tanya asks, her tone admiring. You've met her type before. Groupies who think they want what you wish to God you didn't have.

Do what? you say, because you're not sure if the boy knows. You'd like to think he wouldn't care, but you don't want to scare him away in case he's interested in you as something more than a canvas.

You've only set one fire so far at the high school; thankfully it was in the chem lab. Your partner was more interested in flirting with Mr. Geldon than in helping with your calculations, and you grew frustrated. There were many chemicals on your counter, any combination could have sparked it, but you blamed a faulty Bunsen burner, and everyone pretended to believe.

The rest of your lore is rumor. Some of your cousins don't even know the truth. But Tanya clearly believes.

What thing? the boy says.

She's pyrokinetic, Tanya says, biting a thumbnail and managing to look both disgusted and flirtatious. She sets shit on fire. Why do you think Mr. Bum-Bum has that spray bottle?

Like a firebug? he asks, his eyebrows bunched at the center of his forehead. You want to take two fingers and smooth them back out, one over each eye.

No, Tanya says before you can, tapping her temple. Like Drew Barrymore in that old movie.

The boy's lips purse as if he is about to whistle again. You laugh, but it comes out like a hairball. Heh-heh.

Cool, he says, finally.

Isn't that Mr. Baum? you say, leaning past the curb. It's not.

Give us a demonstration, Tanya says. Her face is flushing up all red. She has probably wanted to say this all year, but this is the last week of Driver's Ed. You have tried not to think about it as the last time. You will miss the boy's Sharpies gliding on the back of your hand. Plus, there's the actual driving, which you need to practice. You are supposed take your test in June, if you can't find a way to put it off.

I'm not giving shows, you say.

But you can really do it? he says. It's genuine interest; you see the change.

A rush of pride trips up your spine. You free your ponytail to tangle in the wind. Yeah, you say, I can.

The thing is, you've never done it on purpose. The bursts mostly come in inconvenient moments, the way you've heard boys get erections in Biology.

Cool, he says again, smiling as if he always knew you were special and now has proof.

Show us at the dance on Saturday, Tanya says. You're going, right?

You point to Mr. Baum's car as if you didn't hear her. He tools closer at a snail's pace, and by the time he pulls up, Tanya's face is its usual implacable mask.

The car smells like an ashtray, which accounts for his tardiness. He has lectured windily about the perils of smoking while driving. Tanya takes the wheel. In the backseat, the boy chews on the cap of a Sharpie, then tugs your wrist into his lap and starts to draw.

Margaret is crying when she gets home on Friday, the day before the dance. Since you belong to no clubs, and Margaret plays field hockey, is VP of SGA, and heads up Amnesty International, SADD, and the Yearbook Committee, you always get home first.

She drops her bag in the living room, where you are napping with a dog-eared copy of *Jane Eyre* on your lap, and goes back outside, sobbing noisily.

What happened? you ask, following her groggily to the front steps.

Nothing, she says, her voice thick as she watches the ascending tide slap the jetty beside your house.

It's been two weeks with no fits, not including the petunias, so she can't be mad at you. You sit next to her. Does everyone at school know about me? you ask.

Margaret stops crying to suck in a breath. Yes, she says. Most of them.

I thought so, you say.

Really it shouldn't matter. The only thing you've wanted from high school since it started is for it to end. When it finally does, you've thought about studying to be an actress. After all, every day is an act for you. It occurs to you now, though, that life might be easier if you could just stop pretending to be normal.

Margaret is still crying. You put your hand on her shoulder.

Hey, you say, what's going on?

She looks at you through a film of tears. Rodney and I broke up, she says.

You slide your arm around her, but she won't give in to your hug. You feel so protective of your sister—she's small, like your mother, but usually so self-assured—that a burst snicks to life inside you, small and contained as a Zippo's flame.

What happened? you ask. Yesterday you were texting him dress swatches to match your corsage. What did Dicken Little do?

It's so typical, Margaret nearly roars, hands buried in her hair. I can never count on him, not for anything. He's not even running the snack table now, and I'm handing out rings all night. No one else can be trusted with the rings.

You have time to be grateful Margaret didn't get your disease. Otherwise, half of your town would be in cinders. Then the burst resurges, trickling upwards, anti-gravity. Your fingertips tingle, your eyes burn.

He cheated, didn't he? you ask. That asshole. That prick. The burst fills you like a bubble blown inside a tin can. Except this bubble wants to tear you open.

Margaret shakes her head no quickly, too quickly, which means yes.

I'll kill him, you say, calm despite what's building inside you.

You're against the death penalty, and violence in general, so you wouldn't really *try*, of course. But you've hated Rodney since you picked up the landline and heard him call you a sideshow freak. True, Margaret told him to take it the fuck back, and he did. But still, the next time you see him, you might not be able to control yourself. You try to breathe in on a four count.

God, don't say that. Do some meditation crap, Margaret says, eyes now dry. O-om-whatever it is. Say the words.

You try, hard, but your sister, your best ally, water to your fire, yin to your out-of-control yang, sits next to you with raccoon-ish eyes because of Rodney "Just Call Me Long Rod" Marshall.

I shouldn't have told you, she says, standing in a new panic. You can't kill him. I don't care about Alicia, or whatever the slut's name is. He's not worth killing. He's not worth anything.

Then you are gripping something inside yourself very, very hard. You close your stinging eyes and listen for the familiar hiss-pop of a fire, but there is nothing except the smack of the screen as Margaret goes inside. Since all your fires are local—within a ten-foot radius—and no one is in sight, it would be okay to let go now. Instead you clench harder, riding the curve of the bubble, letting that unbearable pressure build until you are balanced on its crest, and for the first time in your life, you don't let go.

For a moment you fear your eyes will be expelled from your head, the way you've heard they would be if you held them open during a sneeze. At the height of your distress, even though your fits have never left a mark on you, you have to pinch yourself to confirm that you have not *become* the fire, and then—the closest thing to a miracle since your mother saved you during that first fit you barely remember because she has the scars, not you—your personal inferno subsides.

It hurts like, well, like fire, but after a minute you can breathe without gasping, and when you peek at the world, you see no flames. It's your first averted fire. You've done it. Shown it who's boss. You feel like crying. Like celebrating. You are on your feet before you remember Margaret is mad, but you rush in to tell her anyway.

She is face down on the couch, curiously still.

I did it! I swallowed the burst, you nearly shriek.

She sits up, blinking. You did what?

I'll run the table, you say, though it means you won't be able to dance. Let me do refreshments, you say.

She peels herself up from the couch. Really? she says. You think you can do it?

When you nod, she grabs your hands and the two of you jump up and down until your mother walks in, yawning. She's wearing a tank top, the pinkish scar tissue on her upper arms exposed.

Margaret tells her what you did.

I knew it, your mother says. Hormones.

At the dance, your classmates look like beautiful strangers, hair done and shoes shiny. Margaret has managed to transform the gym into a ballroom with a roll of craft paper for a red carpet and a few artful clutches of silver balloons. Low lighting illuminates couples grinding on each other in a dazzling sea of sequins against suede, satin against silk. It doesn't even matter that most of what you see is flammable.

Of course, you mainly have eyes for Sharpie Boy, who already danced once with a girl on the swim team. Her hair was brown and thin, and you imagined it going up like a mentholated Kleenex before regaining control, easily and with pride. Since yesterday's snuffed fit, you've reveled in your new, delicious ability to pull up short at all your self-imposed stop signs.

Though you are afraid you may not talk to Sharpie Boy, never mind dance with him, at the snack table you are a minor goddess of all you survey. When the dancers are thirsty, they must push wrinkled dollars into your hands. You feel so free and easy that you don't mind repeating the price over and over, and pretend not to see a flask tucked in the suit coat of one of your most frequent customers. Across the gym, Margaret gives you a thumbs-up, which you return. With all your heart, you believe the paper runway safe from your wrath.

Even if Rodney shows, you feel confident you can stay cool.

Taylor Swift is scolding another imperfect ex when Tanya and her friends sidle up. You fill four cups of punch for them, submerging the ladle in the punch's red depths, avoiding floating orange slices.

Her? says one of Tanya's friends in an eighties prom dress with a swatch of black lace over her face.

Your face fills with an ordinary blush. Thankfully, the dance floor's roving red spotlights can't reach you.

You hold out the last cup of punch to Tanya, but she doesn't take it.

When are you going to do it? Tanya says. You know, poof.

You owe Tanya nothing but the punch in your hand, and tell her so.

We won't tell anyone it was you, Tanya says, reaching at last for the cup, swirling the contents against the plastic. Just light up a streamer, Tanya says. We paid ten bucks to get in.

Yeah, we won't tell, Lace Face says in a way that lets you know they've already spread the word.

When a boy cuts through their crowd for a brownie, Tanya's gang drift away, shaking their heads like you are a promising shih tzu that peed on the judge.

Adios, girls, you think, just as Sharpie Boy bellies up to the table in a blue shirt and yellow tie.

There you are, he says.

You blush again, furiously, fighting an inkling of a burst that you soothe handily.

Here I am, you say, leaving one hand on the table so he can see the faint impression of his last drawing—a desert island complete with palm tree and shark's fin. Are you having a good time? you ask.

It's nice to see everyone dressed up, he says, looking only at you.

You bite your cheek to keep from smiling too broadly.

Can you dance later? he asks.

I'm supposed to stay here, you say, though when he looks down, you say, Maybe my sister can cover for me.

He gives you his sweet half-smile. One punch, please, he says. Top shelf.

It's on me, you say, which you hope he recognizes as code for I-like-you.

He grins, bumping into your next customer, who is so familiar that you smile before remembering his crime, and that he's supposed to be running this table. You look around for Alicia What's-Her-Name.

You've got some nerve, you hear yourself say.

Rodney lifts his hands in surrender. Whoa, he says, I was just trying to thank you for taking the table.

Thank me? Does this mean you and Margaret are back together? you say.

He squints like you just spoke Swahili. You scan for Margaret, but she is conveniently missing.

Long Rod backs away now, hands still raised. Mags said you volunteered, he says, then adds, Forget I said anything.

But you can't forget, because Margaret lied. She knew you were coming to the dance and wanted to keep you from having fun. She even fake cried. The fact that she's a better actress than you is the final straw.

Leaving your station for the first time all night, you storm across the gym. Halfway there, Margaret's gaze snags on yours, and her eyes widen with revelation. By the time you reach her, she's cowering amid a clump of friends who disperse on your arrival. "Stairway to Heaven" strains through the speakers, and though you see Sharpie Boy heading back to your empty table, you don't abandon your mission.

Rodney cheated, huh? You lied to me, you say.

I was protecting you, she says, her smile solicitous. You don't know, but slow dancing gets, well, intense.

While you guess this is partly true, the truth is she was also protecting herself, plus her precious dance. With a lie. She tricked you, manipulated you, when your family is supposed to be your safe zone. It's Margaret's job to watch out for you at school; at home you and your sister make sure your mother doesn't drift back into the depression that's almost killed her several times—after you almost killed her, that is—and you protect them all by sitting for hours in a full lotus and counting backwards and never feeling anything fully.

You cried, you say. You never cry.

Yeah, and you swallowed a burst, she says. Remember?

This is also true, but you can't remember that feeling. Your needle is ticking into the red.

Shit, shit, shit, you say, nails buried in your palms.

You can stop it, right? Margaret says, hands fluttering near you without landing. Just swallow it again.

Not this time, you say, and you are sorry, but you don't say so.

You stumble for the door, arms pinwheeling for balance in your borrowed heels. Outside, the humid air offers no relief. You wobble down the steps, the metal railing softening to memorize your fingerprints, and rip off your heels halfway down. In the parking lot, tar sticks to your bare soles, but you don't stop running.

Not a car, you think, anything but a car. As you streak through the lot seeking any private corner, a column of orange flames up from a trash can, barely denting the fit's intensity. You haven't felt a burst this strong since your baby days, when your condition first presented. You don't remember that first time, except you remember it all in a way, because it is family lore, a secret bigger than your own horrible curse.

You run past some kids by the track shed. Rodney's back is to you, and his tie begins to smoke as you pass, but he only pats it with the flat of his hand, examining the cherry on his joint. You try to hold back the bulk of your fit a little longer, remembering a sunny morning when you stood at the bars of your crib, drooling onto a hand-me-down shirt of Margaret's reading Daddy's Little Angel. You couldn't speak except for a stream of Mamamas. The crib was in your mother's room where she was napping, something she did most of the day. Your sister was too young to be outside alone, but she was out in the sandbox anyway.

You were hot in the sun that striped your crib, and hungry. You tried to wake your mother with crying, then with a string of Mamamas. Everyone in your family now knows the term "post-partum depression," as well as several other varieties. Then you only knew you wanted to wake her up.

Her smooth eyelids enraged you. You see them as you run on feet bleeding, tar-spotted, and sore. Weeds in the cracks of the neglected pavement erupt into flame as you pass. You cannot stop to put them out. There is a loading dock near the cafeteria. The dock has a corrugated metal door in a concrete courtyard. It's a place that might save you. As you run, tears sizzle and evaporate from your cheeks on contact.

Mamama, you'd cried. Mamama. She remained still until you realized she wasn't sleeping after all. She was positioning a bed pillow over her head. To block you out. As if you didn't exist. You thought none of this exactly, and all of it at once. Your rage escalated as only a toddler's can, exponentially, a burning sensation tickling the soles of your tiny feet. At the height of your loudest wail yet, a blanket of fire swept across your mother's bed, covering her like a comforter. The one memory you are sure is authentic to this experience is seeing your mother stare out at you, more surprised than scared, from a halo and necklace made of fire.

You cried her name—that string of Mamamas—and she flipped herself onto the ground, snuffing the worst of the flames, then scooped you from the crib, where your skin seared hers like a sunburn. The carpet had started to smolder. The dresser was catching. Downstairs, she grabbed the cordless and ran out back where Margaret sat in the sandbox, pointing at the column of smoke billowing from your parents' window.

The fire department saved the first floor. The second floor is an addition.

Your mother spent a month in the burn unit. She's never blamed you, but that hasn't kept you from blaming yourself. You should have stayed home tonight. It was selfish to want Margaret's kind of life.

Ahead of you, a rusty school bus sits up on blocks. The loading dock is beyond it. As you run, gum wrappers spark and flicker by your ankles. You are fooling yourself that you can swallow the burst in the courtyard, that it's not too late, when a hand grazes your shoulder before its owner draws back with a hiss.

Jessica? your Sharpie Boy says, but when you turn, his eyes widen and the words wither on his lips.

Go away, you say, frantic at his proximity.

No, he says, surprising you into silence, and then before you can warn him, thinking hot—hot—hot, he leans forward, stupidly unafraid, and you have no time to worry about melting his face off because instead of placing his lips on yours, he purses them to blow a cool breeze across your mouth, an anti-kiss. You part your lips and let the cool sweep in like a breath mint, rushing from your nostrils as steam. He's done it, somehow. Distracted you enough to slow the fit.

You feel some slack in the burst and let out a breath, but when you open your eyes, he gives you his sweet half-smile and you realize no one has dared come this close in a fit except for the first time. No one's touched you on purpose. You've assumed that in the whole of your life, no one would. And now you are defenseless. Knowing one person, at least, is brave enough—or dumb enough—to accept you as you are pushes you over the fiery edge.

You both jump when the rusty old bus on its blocks disappears in an undulating orange cloud. He forgets and scalds his fingers pulling you away by your wrist. I'm sorry, you say, retreating on ruined feet as flames the color of clementines peel paint from the side of the bus. Streaks of red and yellow and blue lick the inside of the metal-frame windows.

Don't be, he says. It's beautiful.

Sweat runs off his face from your nearness as much as from the fire devouring the machine before you. Watching your handiwork at the front of the gathering crowd, you know you were right to come out tonight after all. Whether you are in control of your destiny or whether you never will be, you know you're done trying to hide.

Welcome to Snow

Before the baby, Arlene was so thin her hipbones showed. Her hair fell blue-black past her shoulders, and she was always busy with a ring to twirl or a belt to cinch or an eyelash to dig out of her eye so when she took the time to talk to you it made you feel important. This was the year my brother kept inviting her over and then leaving suddenly to take care of "the business," transferring something in a plastic Baggie—wisps of green, wisps of white— from his metal tackle box to his pocket and shuffling out the door without a wave.

At those times Arlene was stuck with me. Two years older, she was infinitely cooler than anyone else I knew. We'd hike behind my house—a three-bedroom deal in the shadow of the Bourne Bridge assaulted by the constant sound of traffic—to where crab grass met scrub pine. The trash train ran through the woods between us and the Cape Cod Canal. We never went to the scenic bike path. Too many joggers and tourists with strollers, plus the occasional streaker.

Next to Arlene, I was the first to know about the baby. The day she told me, early September something, she was smoking cigarettes and I had a pack of cloves even though Spacey Sputner had claimed at lunch they gave you black lung. Not only had the pack cost ten bucks, but I hated Spacey Sputner, who was my only real competition for class valedictorian. That day the bridge above us was quiet in the lull before rush hour.

"Poor Mrs. Ferguson," Arlene said, one foot tapping a second-growth scrub, startling a light rain of needles. I knew she meant the black-and-white dress our calculus teacher had worn.

I choked on a lungful of sweet-smelling vapor. "Jesus," I said. Arlene and I had math together because I was advanced and she was behind. "She was making me seasick."

When Arlene laughed, my knees hummed and tingled. She had a way of making me forget the loner I normally was. I sent up a prayer that she and Simon would never break up.

The cigarettes were my brother's. Arlene had dug them out of the fetid dark of his sock-smelling room, because, unlike me, and for reasons unknown, she wasn't afraid of him. But she didn't have memories of him as a kid, when he was gentle. Around eighth grade, he'd seen all the other boys poised to fill out like water balloons and panicked because he had our father's stringy build. When weights weren't enough, he started buying pills, then selling some, among other things. Arlene knew about the steroids. She said he used them safely, in cycles. Freshman Bio told me his voice might get high, and he risked liver cancer, but the only surface effects were bowling-ball biceps, a short fuse, and ugly grunts when he lifted in the basement.

The clove made my lips taste sweet and sad like a brown leaf crushed underfoot. Despite Spacey Sputner's know-it-all claim, I liked them because they were a no-calorie treat. I was set on making my hipbones push through my school skirt like Arlene's. While my father was a classic beanpole, my mother was Rubenesque. I took after her, but I figured if my brother could mold himself into muscle and toughness, it was possible for me to go the other way. Arlene showed me yoga moves sometimes, downward-dogging with a lit cigarette between her lips.

In the woods, before Arlene's news shattered the day, I was thinking about Peter Allston, Sacred Heart's personal Tom Brady, and the car ride home. Simon had driven with Arlene in the front, as usual, but the backseat was shoulder-to-shoulder football players. "Peter has lap space," Arlene had said, snapping her gum. He'd blushed, but moved his bag so I could sit.

Peter was an okay quarterback, and cute enough, but weirdly shy. He sometimes stuttered. Simon, on the other hand, was the best middle linebacker Sacred Heart had ever seen. Everyone at school called him Girth. Despite abysmal grades, he'd been approached by a couple of scouts. The one he liked best was from The Ohio State University. I had two more years to perfect my escape plan, which could only involve an academic scholarship. No matter what, I wasn't getting stuck here like my parents, who'd never lived anywhere else.

In the woods, Arlene dragged and let it whoosh out. "I'm pregnant," she said, simply.

A semi screamed over the bridge above us, erasing all thoughts of Peter and his lap under my thighs, the way the bare skin on my legs had come alive from hip to ankle.

"What are you going to do?" I asked. Arlene was Catholic, like my family, so I figured she'd keep it, but I couldn't see Simon welcoming a newborn. If he could pull up his grades, he was sure to land a spot on some D-1 institution's elite defensive line next year. I was scared for her, no matter what she decided.

Arlene pinched her cigarette between her fingers, staring at it before grinding it out on the wooden bottom of her clog. It left a black smudge, like a freckle that should be checked for melanoma. I did the same with my clove, and we buried our filters in wet leaves.

"What did Simon say?" We walked back, hugging our elbows against the chill. I was glad I hadn't mentioned Peter. What had happened in the car paled before this new disaster.

"He doesn't know yet," she said.

The world acted like teenage pregnancy was no big news. TLC packaged it up to make it seem as entertaining as *The Voice*.

But I was walking next to a pregnant teen. Inside her was a new life, blind, curled up like a hibernating gerbil, its beating heart the size of a pencil eraser beneath pinkly translucent skin. She lived with her grandparents and two brothers on Cotuit Road. Their mother had checked out years ago, coming back every three years to visit.

"I freaked you out," she said, biting at the skin around a fingernail. "I'm sorry."

When I licked my lips, the clove's sweetness had gone. "Are you guys getting married?"

"I don't want you to worry, okay?" Her face stretched tight when she smiled.

When we emerged from the woods, Simon was smoking in a plastic patio chair, dragging a sneaker against water-stained concrete. Arlene sat on his lap so the chair legs splayed out.

He tossed an empty pack of cigarettes at her chest. "You take some of my smokes?"

She looked down at the pack in her lap. I'd seen him swing at my father for changing the channel from ESPN to PBS. Dad had sidestepped and ordered Simon to take a walk and cool off. In the end, that's what had happened, but I couldn't forget the shape of Simon's fist—big around as a coffee can—cutting a swath through the air. Over one missed double play.

"What's yours is mine," she said. My heart hollowed out, waiting for him to dump her, baby and all, to the ground. Instead he took her bottom lip in both of his. She kissed him back.

Peter Allston had nice lips, full and never chapped. I'd never been kissed and could only imagine what it might feel like, though the car ride today had given me some idea.

I slipped into the house through the slider. My mother was making a chicken pot pie.

"Homework done?" she asked.

I felt bad because of the announcement in her future. We'd

been close when I was young, but we'd drifted apart. Since I was the good one, she left me alone.

"I did it during free," I said, thinking it was Simon's grades she should worry over.

In my room, I lay down and closed my eyes until I could feel again Peter's knees fitting neatly into the space behind my own, the vibrations of the uneven road, the two of us jouncing along together. Faintly I heard Arlene's laugh in the backyard and knew she hadn't told him yet.

Pregnant Sacred Heart girls had to trade uniform skirts for track pants. This was supposedly for comfort but doubled as a scarlet letter. My brother's friends surrounded Arlene like an armed escort when the news got out in mid-September. Boys I knew as the Rickster and Big Dave as well as just plain Peter Allston buffered her from swinging doors, from sympathetic teachers with their hands out to cop a feel, from frantic freshmen spilling around corners grasping ballpoint pens and compasses like spears.

Peter nodded when I passed him on Arlene duty, but despite being in the same chemistry class—him in the back, me in the front—we hadn't talked since that day in the car, weeks before. Still, my body was acutely aware of him whenever we were in the same room. In Chem, I'd look back during a lecture on covalent bonds to see him picking his teeth with a paper clip. At football games I watched him freely from the bleachers. I decided the day in the car had been a fluke, the spark our bodies had struck nothing but an accidental, automatic, biological response.

Arlene's transition into our house began slowly. By the first week of October she was staying for dinner every night, talking brightly and running her silken ponytail through her hand. After dinner sometimes Simon would drive her home. Others, she'd stay and watch TV, picking at her nails on the loveseat, offering fashion advice to the *Real Housewives* of wherever.

Space was tight at her grandparents' place. They had their hands busy with Arlene's brothers, one in eighth grade and one in sixth, who'd been left, like Arlene, when their mother had climbed onto the back of a boyfriend's Harley and split. There was never a decision for Arlene to move in with us, but we had plenty of food on our dining room table, and she liked the chores I despised, singing Joni Mitchell songs over the vacuum in a brave and wild soprano.

More of her stuff appeared in the house every day, a downy white comforter that spent the day behind the couch, a teddy bear with hot pink fur, some books, her toothbrush, her Oxford uniform shirts. The week before Halloween, my mother brought up the green cot from the basement and left it in my room.

The first Tuesday in November, the night before the biggest Chem test of the semester, I came home from school to find Arlene on her cot with a washcloth on her eyes and a pink plastic tub on the floor, empty, beneath her. "Not feeling so well?" I asked.

Just the effort of lifting her head to look at me sent her coughing and sputtering over the tub. "I'm sorry," she said between spasms.

I patted her back, sending frantic mental signals to my mother, but no one came.

"It's fine," I said, forcing my teeth to unclench. I wanted to be the kind of person who didn't mind dropping everything to care for her, but I really needed to study. It was dark by the time she slept.

So I wouldn't wake Arlene, I took my book and flash cards to the dining room table. A flicker of light on the patio brought me to the door and then outside where my mother sat smoking on the back patio, encased in a parka lined with fake fur. There was a lit candle on the table from the hurricane drawer, and a Stieg Larsson book in her hand.

"I don't understand why she can't sleep in with Simon," I said. "What harm could it possibly do now?" My feet on the cold concrete were bare.

"I thought you two were friends," my mother said.

"We are," I said. My stomach turned with disloyalty. She was really my best friend, outside of my books. "She just needs, I don't know, a mother—"

"Maggie," my mother said, steadying a glass of wine she had balanced on her leg. The cigarette jittered almost imperceptibly in her cold fingers. "This wasn't in anyone's plan."

"Are they getting married?" I asked. "Is Simon dragging her to East Boondock State?"

"Until he gets his grades up, he's not going anywhere," she said, which wasn't an answer.

I wanted my mother to act like she cared. She and my father had Simon right after high school, which had put all her plans on hold indefinitely. Once, after too many glasses of wine that I kept sneaking sips of, she told me her greatest dream as a little girl was to join the navy and sail all around the world. After Simon was born, she took a job as a secretary in a nursing home *for the time being*, and she worked there still, seventeen years later.

"Aren't you disappointed?" I asked.

My mother turned a page. Behind her was the dark window of her bedroom, where my father was asleep already. "What's done is done," she said, ashing over the concrete.

"I can't work. Don't you care about my grades?" A TV from the Parsons' house blared a rerun of *The Tonight Show* and what I really wanted was to fold myself into a parka, pour my own glass of wine, and study by her candle.

"You'll do just fine," my mother said, staring into her glass as if she could read pulverized grape flesh like tea leaves. "You always do."

A barge moaned by in the canal, and I shivered. If it was me who'd gotten pregnant, I wondered if she would be so calm, take so little responsibility. But I was a careful girl. She thought she didn't have to worry about me. I stood out there a minute longer, waiting for her to look up at me, or say goodnight, squeeze my wrist, smile.

Simon drove us to school early the next morning to meet a new tutor his coach had found. His hand swallowed my elbow before I could get out. "You have Chem with Allston?"

I froze. The day in the car was two months ago now, but what if Peter had said something and now Simon was pissed? Just last July I'd seen my brother put his fist through the kitchen window because my mother told him to stop sneaking beers. "Yeah," I said. "So?"

"Give him this," he said, producing a white envelope from his back pocket. He let go of me then and got out, circling the car to open Arlene's door. I'd never seen him do that before.

Everyone was early to Chem, their noses close to the formulas as if trying to inhale the mysterious combinations of numbers and letters. I was the only sophomore in the class. Otherwise it was all juniors and a few seniors who'd skipped it last semester, or had failed out. My brother had managed a C+ last year, but a few of his friends were in it now as seniors. Peter Allston had ear buds in, so a faint whine of Incubus clung to him like static electricity.

"Here," I said, dropping the envelope on his desk. "From my brother."

"Girth was supposed to give these to me last night, so I had time to look them over," Peter said. There was an empty seat next to him. Though I usually sat in the front, I took it, watching him slide five thin strips of paper covered in writing out of the envelope. He sorted them on his desk, glancing up to make sure Ms. Clemson still hadn't arrived. With a roll of tape from his pocket, Peter attached the first strip to his pencil, showing me how if he cupped his hand right it couldn't be seen. "You probably studied your ass off. Or maybe you don't need to."

It was social suicide to admit to liking school. "I couldn't," I said. "Arlene was sick."

"You took care of her?" he asked, looking up. "That's really sweet."

I recited molecular formulas to calm my heart. AuBr, gold bromide; CH_3OH, methanol; H_2O, good old water.

"Not really," I said, but Ms. Clemson had come in and my voice was lost in the flurry of last-minute questions.

Though I hadn't had to ride on a lap since that day two months ago, I thought about it almost daily. That afternoon the Rickster had been up against the far rear window, running his tongue over his lips for a passing pair of freshman girls. Big Dave's big laugh echoed in the Buick. "Imbeciles," Arlene said into the mirror, picking lipstick off her teeth. Meanwhile I sat sideways on Peter's lap. It was cramped. My head grazed the roof, and I'd had to hold Arlene's headrest to stay upright.

Peter shifted me around until his knees were under my knees. "You all in?" he said.

I'd looked back at him, over my shoulder. He had two freckles to the right of his mouth and on his chin a tiny forest of honey-colored bristles. "Yeah," I said, and he'd closed the door.

My shirt billowed loose over my skirt. Peter's fingers played a lefty piano on the side of his knee, twitching my skirt until my legs prickled into goosebumps. Thigh to ankle, their lengths felt unconnected to me, anecdotal, but crackling with possibility.

We were almost to Dave's house, our first stop, before Peter's fingers slid between the bottom of my thigh and the top of his. Slowly, so slowly. I dipped my chin to my right shoulder, looking back at his uptilted face. He stopped, waiting for permission. The other guys were arguing about the greatest running back in the NFL, Adrian Peterson or Chris Johnson. They were distracted. Still, it was all-over wrong. My *brother* was in the car. It was sick, even, but I didn't want him to stop. I tried to nod, giving my okay, and brushed my forehead against Arlene's headrest. She must have felt it, because her eyes caught on mine in the side mirror.

I didn't know then she was carrying the burden of those E.P.T. tests. All I knew was Peter's fingers began moving again, inching in and back until one brushed the pilled elastic at the edge of my underwear. He stopped again, as if I might change my mind, but I only gripped Arlene's headrest and shifted a little to the right. Those panties were the oldest pair I owned. He didn't seem to mind.

By then my nerves were high tension wires, and parts of me were pulsing that had been asleep my whole life. I was still gripping the headrest, eyes closed, holding my breath without meaning to, taken over by the warmth that pooled between us now, and what felt like a delicate gathering of golden fibers drawn to the place Peter's finger was slowly tracing, when Simon jerked to a stop in front of Big Dave's house. "Someone let me out of this deathtrap," Dave said.

I panicked, reaching for the door handle and spilling into the driveway on the verge of something I had only heard about, secondhand, at sleepovers. Peter gasped as I slid off, and followed me into the driveway, turning away from the car, but not before I'd seen the bulge in his jeans. It made me glad to know the warmth had worked both ways.

I waited to be discovered, but all that happened was Big Dave trotted up the path to his house and Peter asked me to grab his backpack. "Think I'll walk home from here," he called over his shoulder. He took his bag without touching me. "Sorry," he whispered, jogging away before I could ask if he was sorry he started it or sorry he didn't finish.

"Our next game is at home," Peter said now, in class, under buzzing fluorescents. I blinked to see our test rolling toward us as the students in the front each took a sheet and passed it overhead. I focused on the rustling of paper. "You should come, if you want."

"Maybe I'll try to make it," I said, smiling wider than I meant to.

The chain reaction he ignited in me then was as irreversible as the one that had taken place in Arlene's body, even if we didn't make any sense. Peter was a catch. I was medium pretty. He dreamed of the NFL, and my heart thrilled to decipher word problems. I tried to see myself as he did, a short girl with wavy brown hair. Skirt riding high on pale thighs, bare legs in brown loafers. I could only chalk it up to pheromones and the mystery of human preference that Peter—who would never see the beauty I saw in numbers—only had to smile to set part of me aglow.

Ms. Clemson's exams had landed on our desks, each white as the foam atop a wave.

"Good luck," I said, some instinct tilting my head for me, biting my lip.

"Don't need it," he said, winking and twirling his doctored pencil between his fingers.

Even though I finished the test before Peter, I checked and rechecked my answers, waiting to leave until he dropped his test in the pile at the front.

"Brutal," he said in the hallway. "I'd be dead if it wasn't for your delivery."

"I could have used some 'study aids' myself," I lied. The hour had flown by for me in a satisfying blur.

Peter nodded. "I just pray I pulled a C."

"Good luck with that," I said, so we could laugh. He was concerned with passing, not excelling. But when I escaped, it wouldn't be because of my explosive forty-yard passes.

"Maggie," he said. We were at the top of a set of stairs, me poised to go down. Girls in plaid and boys in khaki parted and rejoined around us. I stepped closer, so only the width of my textbook kept us apart. He pushed a crisp piece of paper into the breast pocket of my Oxford shirt, his fingers lingering there a beat longer than necessary. "Tell Girth thanks for me, okay?"

I nodded, then made myself wait until Calculus to pull out the paper with trembling fingers. It was only the envelope that had held the cheats, blank on both sides, but I remembered the pressure of his fingers and knew what it meant all the same.

My brother used to have a thing for *Star Wars*. A suitcase under his bed still holds all the figures he used to collect, little plastic Boba Fetts and Darth Vaders and frog-faced Jabba the Hutts. *Star Wars* was the thing my brother did with Dad until high school hit and

Simon sidestepped into a world of football practice and weekend keggers and blow jobs in the janitor's closet I wish the rumor mill had never revealed. By the time I was a sophomore in high school, the thing he did with my dad was fix stuff in the basement, like the furnace once, and the odd wobbly chair. When they had a project, I brought them down their dinner.

A night in late November, when Arlene had gone to bed early, I took two plates of pork chops and green beans into the saw-dust-smelling basement. They had the Patriots on the radio.

"Stellar," my father said when I wedged his plate on a corner of the workbench. With his narrow face and owl-eye glasses, my father looked more like a professor than an electrician. My brother outweighed him by fifty pounds of pure muscle. The neighbors might have circulated some mailman jokes, but pictures of them at twelve made them look like twins.

"Your mother never puts enough salt," my father said. "Back in a flash."

In his absence, I took a green bean off my father's plate. It was al dente, the way I like it.

"Careful, Mags, you're filling out," Simon said, jabbing a finger above my belly button.

"It's a green bean, genius. It has no calories," I said, and he laughed. I couldn't remember how long it had been since we'd joked around. Maybe he was gentling for the baby. "Arlene said you got a B on your history test. Looks like you might graduate after all."

"It's just one test," he said, modest for once. He was on one of the beat-up metal stools, the heels of his Nikes balanced on two different rungs. When I picked up another green bean, he picked up one of his own. "En garde," he said, and brandished the bean, thrusting until I parried. We'd had lightsaber wars in the back-yard when we were younger, our battles made dramatic by the whooshing of cars on the bridge above. The current battle ended when he chomped my bean in half. We laughed at the stub between my fingers, and then he plucked that up and ate it too.

At the home game last Saturday, Arlene and I had sat together, sharing a blanket on the metal bleachers. Peter looked our way once from the field, but he didn't seem to see me in the crowd. I'd wanted to tell Arlene that I thought Peter liked me, but I didn't want to jinx it. Nothing had really happened yet. She spoke first, though. "I barely recognize him out there," she said, and there was no need to ask who she meant. Simon was screaming and beating his own chest with fists the size of cantaloupes, hollering into the wind, biceps testing his Spandex uniform, veins standing out like tree roots in the reddened flesh of his neck. He was a monster.

"He just gets hyped up for the games," I'd said, wanting to believe that's all it was.

In the basement now, I couldn't forget her eyes widening as if seeing him for the first time.

"You're going have to keep The Hulk away from the baby, you know," I said. My limbs filled immediately with ice. Simon still pinched his green bean. I wondered if I should be afraid.

He twirled the bean between finger and thumb. There was grease under his nails from the lawn mower he and my father had been reassembling. "Come again?"

His empty hand fisted up against his massive leg. Still holding the bean with the other, he stood, looking down on me from the great height of two years and all the inches he'd grown over me. I think I didn't understand until then the way I would always be younger than him. Our father started back down the stairs. I heard him whistling over the thumping of his steps.

"You heard me, *Girth*," I said, heart rabbiting along. He looked like nobody's father.

"The kid is not your business. Arlene is not your business, and neither am I." He still gripped the bean, green and ridiculously erect, between his right index finger and thumb. He stood and swept the stool against his bench press, where it rang out cheerfully and fell unharmed.

"What's going on?" my father asked, taking the last stairs two at a time.

"Nothing," Simon said. I saw his face go red as a newborn's before he sunk into a squat.

"Go on up now, Mags," my father told me quietly, returning the stool to its feet.

"You're scary," I told Simon before I went up, tensing for a blow that never came.

Simon and I made our peace by Christmas, but I still didn't trust him around me or the baby-to-be, due on one of those days steeped in incense and tradition between Palm Sunday and Easter. We all stayed in on New Year's Eve, since Arlene couldn't propel herself out of pj's.

"Why don't you take the bed instead of the cot from now on?" I asked, winding down from a sparkling cider sugar high. It was snowing small, hard flakes that tinked against my bedroom window. I'd grown to like her presence in the dark. It was like having a sister.

"No thanks, Mags," she said. "Maybe when I'm too fat to hoist myself up anymore."

I wondered if Simon's drugs did bad things to their baby. I pictured it pink and healthy, made of springy clean flesh except for the tips of its toes, which were stained a moss green. Or maybe the baby was perfect on the outside, but inside, invisible fingers busily popped brain cells like soap bubbles. It bothered me that Arlene never seemed to worry. Her placid acceptance was too much like my mother's must have been when Simon's appearance canceled her best dreams.

We skipped school on Valentine's Day, Arlene and I. It fell on a Friday anyway. My mother just nodded when I told her I felt sick, and Arlene didn't have to say anything. She was big, almost eight months gone, and was always putting my hand on her belly to feel the thing move around. I couldn't believe there was a baby in there. The little kicks felt to me like a bag of rocks set to tumble dry. In the morning we watched *The Today Show*, *Judge Judy*, *The Price Is Right*, and *The Tyra Show*, an episode on teenage girls who were trying to get pregnant.

The panelists were twelve to fifteen, or claimed to be. They wore tube tops and miniskirts, black mascara and too much gel. The girl on the end sat with her arms crossed the whole time. "I just want something to love me," she told Tyra, tossing straw-colored hair over her shoulder. "You don't know I won't be a good mom."

I was in the kitchen making ramen noodles, but I could still hear Tyra promising that after the break G.I. Joseph would yell those girls into shape. I-Want-a-Baby Boot Camp would involve sit-ups and mystery meat and a ban on deodorant for a whole weekend.

"What does boot camp have to do with babies?" I asked.

Arlene said, "God only knows. Let's eat outside, I'm burning up."

We took our soup to the glass table on the back patio. It was freezing, piles of dirty snow pushed up against the house and fresh snow coating the seats of our chairs, but we were wrapped in scarves and hats with bobble tops from when Simon and I were kids. The soup streamed white columns that dispersed against the gray sky. I wasn't sure if the combo of cold and hot was good for the baby, but I figured Arlene would know better than me.

"Grammy cries every time I go over to visit," Arlene said. "I don't know why I bother."

I slurped my noodles one at a time, wiping hot broth off my nose. "She's still mad?"

"She just keeps saying babies are so expensive, and that I'm in for a hard road."

Grammy was right, I thought, listening to the traffic on Sandwich Road. Someone next door slammed a car door. My parents were footing her bills now, but how long could that go on?

"What do you think of Peter Allston?" I asked. We'd talked every day in Chemistry for months, but so far that was all.

Arlene drained her bowl. "He's a doofus. But not bad looking." She winked, then struggled to her feet and went inside to put her bowl in the sink. When she got back, my soup was cold.

"I'm dying for a cigarette," Arlene said, rubbing her mittened hands together. It was freezing. Too cold to be outside. Arlene coughed into a mitten. "Are you hot for Peter Allston?"

"Me and a dozen other hopefuls," I said, part of me wishing she'd try and stop me. Say, *Be careful, don't turn out like me.* Show some fucking feeling, cry a little, tell me she was scared.

Instead she grinned. "Did he feel you up in the car?" Some drops of soup had iced over on the table, so I knew the temperature had dropped suddenly, like it can in New England, when you least expect it. "I watched you two in the side mirror. The day you sat on his lap."

"The side mirror," I said, nodding. It started snowing again. We looked up at each other and grinned, letting flakes crowd our eyelashes. The surface of my soup filled with tiny ripples.

"This is snow, Baby," Arlene said, mittened hands cupping her belly. It was the first time I'd heard her talk to the kid. She rubbed her middle, looking up, and said: "Welcome to snow."

We finally went inside because Arlene's lips turned blue around the edges. G.I. Joseph—bald, gap-toothed—was finishing up the boot camp. We put him on mute so we could watch his eyes bug out and his teeth crash up and down. Arlene pretended to calculate the arc of the spit shooting out of his mouth. That was the sort of problem they dealt with in her physics class.

The girls struggled through modified push-ups and cried, cupping their elbows with tiny, soft hands. "They're a bunch of rocket scientists," I said, but Arlene snapped her head up.

"Fucking sad is what they are," she said. "Tyra should give each of them a dog."

We laughed for a while until it turned to tears, and maybe that was what we'd both been waiting for. Arlene said, her eyes streaming, "Fucking Dobermans, man. Great fucking Danes."

We were on the couch, and there was no one home but us, and she sort of rolled on her side so her head fell into my lap. I combed the snow out of her hair, only it had become a cross between slush and just plain water. Arlene put her face in her hands and barely noticed when I slipped out from under her. When I came back with the hair dryer, she was as still as I'd ever seen her, sobbing with her eyes squinched down into slits. I needed an extension cord from the kitchen before I could switch it on. When the hot air hit her face, she opened her eyes.

"It's my hair that's wet, you dumbass," she said, smiling, taking in great gulps of air.

"First things first," I said, and trained the stream on her cheeks where tears had paved a twisted jungle of mascara paths, alternating right to left so she wouldn't get burned.

My brother joined me on the patio the first Saturday in April. Arlene was laid up on my bed with fake labor pains. The baby would be here in six days, though nobody knew that yet.

"Can I get one of those?" Simon said, lowering himself into a chair.

I tossed him my pack. It smelled like Christmas because of the cloves, but the buds on the trees were a misty green, and spring was true to its name, waiting for the right moment to pounce.

"My tutor says my grades are good enough for OSU, barely," he said. "I'm going to send Arlene money every month out of my student loans."

"You're still leaving." The cloves' incense smell reminded me next Sunday was Easter.

He shifted, planting his elbows on his knees. "It was an accident, Mags. They happen."

I took a shallow drag. He was an accident, too. I wonder what it did to him, knowing that.

"I'm sorry," he said. "Is that what you want me to say?"

"Not to me," I said. "Your accident isn't holding me back. Or you, for that matter."

"You want me to be punished," he said, trapping the smoke from his clove in his lungs. It would be dark in there, black, a mine shaft. He shifted in his chair, and I was afraid he'd just stand and leave. As a kid, he always dueled as Luke. I was Darth Vader and lost every fight.

"Yes," I said. "No. I just worry about her here, without you. Don't you love her?"

Simon coughed. "I'll come back some weekends. I'll just be at school."

"Christmas," I said. "Easter."

"You can take over the business," he said, teasing me. "Make a few extra bucks. The tackle box is all yours." All those Baggies folded over harmless-looking pills, herbs, powder.

"Ha, ha," I said, wishing I was a boy so I could hit him and he would know I was serious.

"What do you want from me?" he said. "I haven't done any enhancement for, like, a year. Schools test for that shit. I know I get too angry sometimes, but you act like you hate me now."

There was so much water in the air, I felt like someone had squeegeed a sponge over my head. It was too early for humidity, but there it was all the same. With one hand I swept my heavy hair away from my neck. I wasn't sure what I wanted. It wouldn't make sense to take her and a newborn to college, or to marry her quickly before the kid came if that's not what they wanted. We weren't living in the dark ages. But I still wanted something, some gesture.

"I just want you to do the right thing," I said.

He came back to the table and reached for another clove, shaking one out for me. "That's the thing, Mags. There *is* no right thing, not the way you think there is." He stayed long enough for me to have a fantasy that college would fix him. He'd come back a Jedi, my hero again.

In Chem class Friday, the day Arlene's baby was born, Peter told me he'd chosen UMass.

"That's awesome," I said. "Congrats."

I still didn't know if all our flirting was only in my head, but I'd decided to let him sleep with me, if he wanted to, before he left. Just to see what all the fuss was about.

Arlene was five days past her due date and hadn't been in school all week. Peter rode home in the back behind Simon and me. "She ready to pop yet?" he asked, grinning at no one in particular. I remember looking at him in the rearview, thinking: He is a sweet, dim, beautiful boy.

We were almost home when my brother's phone rang. It was Arlene's grandmother.

"We're at the hospital," I heard her say over the cell, voice crisp and urgent. "Hustle in."

Simon sped the rest of the way. "Get out," he said, his face stricken as if electrocuted.

"But—" Peter said as Simon peeled away, stranding him. He'd have a long walk home.

"Come in a minute. No one's here," I said, my pulse quickening so I could feel it in my wrists. I unlocked the house and gave him a tour that ended in my room.

"Neat," he said, eyeing my bed until I had counted every wrinkle in the quilt. We stood there, me crossing and uncrossing my arms and Peter scratching at the grain of his jeans.

"Arlene is having her baby now," I said. If I wanted to propel us into bed, it was the wrong thing to say, but to break the tension it was the exact right thing.

"Wanna go for a walk?" he asked.

The day was mild, springlike, and once we followed the sidewalk into town and escaped the smell of exhaust, Peter reached down and took my hand. We followed the sidewalk past the library and the baseball field behind it. There was a game on. Little boys in purple against little boys in blue. We passed the pharmacy and the pediatric dentist and the bait shop. We passed the graveyard with its markers yellowed by lichen and mold. Peter would find other girls at college. And that was for the best. I think we both knew I wanted to get farther from home than Amherst.

There was a Cumberland Farms on the corner. We went in for ice cream sandwiches and ate them outside with the curb burning my thighs beneath my school skirt.

Peter licked vanilla off his lips. "I don't know anything about you," he said.

"Okay," I said. I'd eaten my ice cream into a circle. "Sometimes I do yoga in the woods."

He nodded, storing up the information. "That's good," he said. "That's a start."

When his father came to pick him up, Peter kissed me goodbye just as if it had been a real date. His mouth was sweet with ice cream. My brother's message on the machine said Arlene had had a baby girl, seven pounds three ounces, he was holding her in his arms right now. I pictured her alien-headed as an eggplant, black-haired, strong-willed, blue-eyed although that would change, the way everything would. There was a brief cry in the background, like proof.

Straight and Narrow

At first I couldn't help but think of him as the criminal. He chose an apron striped black and white, like the other men in the class, though there were other stripes to choose from: red and white, green and white, blue and white. The class was made up of YMCA junkies, all but the criminal. Last month ceramics, this month me.

Beating eggs in plastic bowls held against their hips, or bending too far into ovens like fairy-tale witches, the women were a flurry of color in pinks and yellows and periwinkle. But the men adopted that strange solidarity. Even the mousiest husbands who kept solicitous hands forever behind the elbows of their wives.

The criminal shared a counter with the Norman newlyweds, and his quick hands were good with a knife. He could reduce a stalk of celery to little green commas in seconds. Fresh out of maximum security at Sing-Sing, a repeat offender but no danger to anyone but himself, he'd told me at registration, now he was just a guy looking for his straight and narrow.

Mrs. Norman stood her ground next to the criminal. She was chatty and short and looked about my age. Early thirties, with hair the color of a cast iron pot.

Also, she was full to bursting with a first child. That was the main difference between us.

During registration I showed them how to make smoothies.

Together we watched the criminal feed bananas to his blender one sickle-shaped fruit at a time.

Week One

"First the hollandaise," I said, moving between counters with their green granite tops.

We'd begun with a guacamole base instead of egg yolk. Husbands mashed avocado cubes while wives apportioned mayonnaise and lime juice, tossed in Tabasco to taste. The criminal hummed while he worked, something bluesy that made me think of dark nightclubs filled with smoke haze.

"We'll have to remember this for Cinco de Mayo," Mrs. Norman said. She was pert and pretty and I doubted she'd ever made it out of Saratoga Springs, never mind to Mexico. To her left, her husband stirred dutifully; to the right, the criminal grinned down at his bowl.

"You know what's funny, most Mexicans don't celebrate Cinco de Mayo," the criminal said. His teeth were even and yellow, a mockery of perfection. His voice ground out like a tire in gravel. "Your average American thinks it's their Independence Day, but that's really September sixteenth."

For a few seconds there was only the symphonic plunge and release of spatulas urging mayonnaise mixtures toward liquidation. The room smelled of vinegar.

Mr. Norman turned his head energetically, leaning across the counter so Mrs. Norman was forced to move back. "That's real interesting, bub," he said. "Where'd you hear that?"

Mrs. Norman placed one hand on her belly, as if to cover the baby's ears.

"Call me Arthur," the criminal said.

We thought of adobe jail cells. Drug cartels. *We don't need no stinkin' badges.*

The criminal held his sauce up for approval. He gripped the sides of his bowl instead of allowing his fingers to hang over the rim. The sauce within had the bubbly appearance of primordial ooze, but on the tongue it was smooth and tangy, an excellent first effort and the best in the class. He smiled like a kid with a gold star while I held out a hand for his paring knife. He gave it to me handle first and our fingertips met at the base of the blade, a quick, rasping touch.

"Step two," I said. "Let's poach some eggs."

Later I fed my husband the leftovers. We sawed at Canadian bacon, dry from the microwave, while a summer sun set behind the lake."Have you ever been to Mexico?" I asked.

He looked up from his paper, the reading of which was his main occupation in the summer months when he was not required to profess. A web of blood vessels had burst on the apples of his cheeks since we'd met half a dozen years ago, a change that made him appear permanently jolly. In the last year, his fingers had started to swell up after eating, so he'd take off his wedding ring for meals. It gleamed next to his plate now, silver and full of refracted light.

"What?" he asked. The Life & Leisure page waffled in the breeze of his breath. Once he'd been my T.A. at the college down the road. He'd studied Freud in Vienna, Rorschach in Switzerland, and he'd promised to take me back there, to show me the world. But first there wasn't money and then there wasn't time.

I thought of thick blue corn tortillas smothered in queso and chile so hot my tongue would pulse in waves. Posole topped with sprigs of cilantro and spiked with a freshly squeezed lime. Hearty bowls of abondigas. Tacos al carbón. Red enchiladas. A sweet caramel flan.

The summer stretched out before us. I said, "Don't you ever want to get away?"

He reached for my hand across the table and brought it to his lips. "Maybe next summer," he said, and then released me.

Week Two

"Start your engines," I said, and thirteen index fingers pushed purée.

Twelve belonged to half a couple of friends or spouses. Just one to a criminal.

I circulated, watching chickpeas turn into paste and encouraging experimentation. A handful of sun-dried tomatoes here, sprinkling of feta there. Another garlic clove. Pinch of salt.

The test kitchen filled with the smell of lemon juice and olive oil, paprika and garlic and mint. I'd wanted Greece for a honeymoon. Spanakopita and baklava. Lamb souvlaki and carafes of piney retsina. Instead, my husband's parents sent us to DisneyWorld, and we'd ridden Space Mountain every day. The two of us hurtling through Tomorrowland at breakneck speeds.

"I bet this will be yummy," Mrs. Norman said. She scooped up a dollop of hummus and licked it, pink tongue darting blink-and-you'll-miss-it fast. Her eyes closed in appreciation. The baby was getting a taste too. She was shaping its likes and dislikes, its cravings, before it ever took a sip of air. She scooped again and held it to her husband, who swallowed, nodding.

"I'll take that bet," the criminal said. His hummus was dished up already, garnished with a pool of tahini and a pair of kalamata olives.

Mrs. Norman faced him, her smile stuttering one second too slow.

Then she dipped the spoon back into her bowl and fed him, watched his lips drag over the place where hers and her husband's had been, and set the spoon clicking to the counter. He closed his eyes when he swallowed, a smile etching lines like parentheses into his leathered face.

"Now, that's good," the criminal said, Arthur, his name was. Licking his lips.

Then, "Fair's fair." He pushed his bowl her way.

Mrs. Norman turned to her husband, her hands gone again to her stomach.

"Oh no," she said, smiling wildly. "Thanks, but I've had enough."

"What's the matter, Lily?" Her husband reached over their own bowl and picked up the spoon, thrice used. "It looks delicious."

She blinked rapidly, the whites of her eyes seeming to swallow all the blue.

Mr. Norman jabbed the spoon into Arthur's bowl and brought it to his wife's mouth.

"Go on, honey," he said. "Try it."

It hovered before her lips, which remained closed while her eyes reddened at their rims.

"Forget about it," Arthur said, smiling with deep wrinkles ringing his eyes. He took a new spoon from the supply drawer and tasted his own handiwork. "Could use some salt."

I was distributing storage containers for take-homes, coming to the Normans' table last.

"Christ on a carousel, Lilith," Mr. Norman said. He thrust the spoonful she'd refused into his own mouth and swallowed violently. "Oh, you're missing out, Lily. That's out of this world."

"A little bland, actually," Arthur said, studying his hands splayed on the counter. Hands that had hurt someone, maybe; wielded a gun; counted a wad of money from some illegal transaction. Hands that were capable of anything, everything, as far as we knew.

His skin had toughened by some force of nature or man, and his dark eyes glinted from a face almost the color of brick. When he pushed the sleeves of his pilled brown sweater up nearly to the elbow, you could see the tattoos done in blue on his forearm. One a Red Cross snake, one the sight of a rifle. One a bulldog with teeth like a mountain range.

He kept his nails neat, his hands clean, and they were strongly muscled, the veins and bones working in concert with the slightest flex. I watched him fingering his spoon, wondered what those fingers would feel like tripping up and down the vertical crevasse in a woman's back. My back. I inhaled slowly through my nose to clear my head and moved to an adjacent table.

The Normans prepared to leave without speaking to each other. She dumped their hummus into a plastic container while he washed his hands halfheartedly at one of the communal sinks. After they left, Arthur and I were left alone in the kitchen. He removed his apron.

"May I?" I asked. He smelled like sun-soaked sawdust, clean and sweet.

He pushed his bowl toward me and stood from his stool, knees cracking like gunshots.

He was right. It was bland. "I'd try some sesame oil and a little black pepper," I said as he filled his container.

"In the Middle Ages, in England, they thought birth defects were the mother's fault. Pregnant ladies weren't supposed to look at cripples or think about the devil, or else their kid would turn out half monster." He set his backpack on the counter and unzipped it to slip in the hummus. The bag was filled with towels and boxers, razors and travel tubes of toothpaste.

I forced myself to look back at his face, that sun-crisped expanse. Close up, he seemed a bit careworn, but you'd never guess he'd lived a total of fifteen years inside a barbed wire fence. I wondered where he'd been before that. Why he was here now.

"But then you've got your Ottomans," he went on, drifting toward the door. "And they used to say if you keep a mother from eating something she craves, the baby comes out with a birthmark on its head in the shape of the food. So there you go."

Assault. Battery. Rape. What had it been? He had such neat hands.

"Do you have somewhere to stay, Arthur?" I asked. It was the first time I'd said his name, and for a heartstopping second I'd almost called him criminal.

"Best Western's putting me up. Work release thing. They give me a room, I work in the laundry," he smiled. "Just like at home."

I had no way of knowing if that's what he'd done before prison or in it.

"It's lunch recipes next week," I said.

"Sounds good, Mrs. M," he said, the "Mrs." rolling around awkwardly in his mouth, and then took off up West Avenue toward Washington. I noticed he wore no wedding ring.

At home, my husband's face turned pink with pleasure at seeing me. I curled into the armchair with him, crinkling the newspaper he'd been reading and kissing a star-shaped pattern against his cheek. "Well, hello yourself," he said, then wiggled out from beneath me and went into the kitchen to dip a triangle of pita into my concoction.

"Too much pepper," he said, and coughed to prove his point. But it didn't stop him from finishing the bowl and licking his pink sausaged fingers.

Later, lying in bed, I watched the streetlight seep in through the window blinds, painting our whole room with narrow bars of gold that I usually counted, slowly, when sleep proved elusive. Tonight, my husband kissed my shoulder. Testing the waters and tasting the salt of me. I turned to him and lifted one of his heavy hands, placing it on my hip, where I warmed immediately. He'd kept his nails long once upon a time to pick the banjo in a bluegrass band. I hadn't asked him to quit after we were married, but he had anyway, and the instrument had been caged up in our attic going on five years.

A strip of light fell across his nose, another over his forehead, leaving his eyes in shadow. We'd planned to go to London one year, for our August anniversary, but terrorists blew up those Tube trains that summer, and he'd convinced me we should cancel our tickets.

"What's so attractive about English cuisine anyway?" he'd asked.

Steaming plates of Sunday roasts and airy Yorkshire puddings. Fish and chips served in grease-soaked sheets of newsprint. English breakfasts with baked beans and bread fried crisp in bacon fat. Bangers and mash. Tea and crumpets oozing butter. Dense, sweet Spotted Dick.

"Most people would say, nothing," I'd said, wondering what the point was of marrying a psychology professor if he couldn't interpret his own wife's mind.

And I wasn't such a mystery. Every place had its own taste. I wanted to sample them all.

"Let's try again," I said now, his hand inscribing slow circles on my lower back, our torsos perfectly aligned. "We could have white truffles in Alba, Tuscan Chianti, gelato in Venice from a sidewalk stand. Let's go to Italy," I said. "Shots of limoncello after every meal."

"Neither of us speaks Italian," he said, laying his lips against my throat, blinking his eyelashes against me in a feathery tickle like what precedes a sneeze. We'd had a five-year plan. See the world, then start a family. But Tomorrowland wasn't enough for me.

"I know," he said. "Let's go down to the city this weekend," he said. New York City. To a native Saratogan, the Big Apple was the only city that mattered. "We'll cruise through Little Italy."

He rolled over then, on top, driving me further into the mattress, working both of us further beneath the covers, and I pictured the bars of light and shadow drawn across the white expanse of his back.

Fresh-baked loaves of ciabatta, flour-dusted in a brick oven. Thick wheels of biting Asiago. Mounds of al dente spaghetti. Hand-shaped tortellini stuffed with Parmesan and spinach. Pizza layered with prosciutto and mozzarella. Trays of warm almond-dotted biscotti. Espresso.

Ciao.

Week Three

In mid-June the heat of summer settled in Saratoga, and with it the tourists, though racing season wouldn't start until the middle of July. In another month the city would double in population, and its roads would seem to shrink by half. Saudi sheikhs would stride the streets in their white *thobes*, cotton *ghutras* swaddling their heads in pure white or red-and-white checks.

Other foreign visitors would be harder to pick out, until you heard them speak at the Price Chopper, lovely elongated vowels and clipped consonants. Ireland and Australia. Germany and Spain. South Africa, Japan, India, Egypt. For two months in the summer the world would come to Saratoga Springs, and then, as if we'd woken from a dream, it would leave.

I wanted to follow the world to its four corners, then bring it back home in my recipe book. Each taste better than a photograph. Proof of a thousand possible lives waiting to be lived.

In class this week, Mr. Norman was without Lily. Arthur noticed before I did. He asked after her over their pans of simmering sausage, the two men catching olive oil splatters on their black-and-white protective garments, gabbing like a pair of referees at halftime.

"A little under the weather," Mr. Norman said. "The heat really gets to her these days."

"Tell me about it," Arthur said. "When my wife was pregnant, she sent away for brochures on Alaska. Until winter hit, and then it was Texas. Somewhere that never cooled off."

I lingered by their counter, but their talk dried up with me there. I inspected the contents of their pans, standing between them so Arthur's body heat was a felt presence against my side.

"Very good," I said to him. "You can take them off now. Slice them into thin rounds."

Mr. Norman's sausages actually looked better, but I remembered him last week, trying to force-feed his wife to assuage his own embarrassment. "You're burning them," I said.

The two men sliced in companionable silence while I handed out premade pie crusts settled into disposable aluminum pans. Two older ladies at the rear counter called me over, and I helped them get the body of their quiche started, cracking four eggs into the mixer, adding the heavy cream, the pepper, the rosemary, the salt.

When I returned to the Normans' table, their talk had moved on to other things.

"I grew up in the city," Mr. Norman was saying. "Now I've got skiing at my doorstep, horse racing every year. I'd never go back."

"It's a little hoity-toity for me," Arthur said, mixing in the cheese and broccoli. I wondered where he'd been born, how far he'd roamed in between. "But my daughter's here, so here I am."

The ovens had reached prime temperature and it was time to put the quiches in, but I wanted to hear a little more. I strolled over with my arms behind my back like a science fair judge, looking down my nose at their counter. I'd loosely tied a silk scarf around my neck today, purchased in the Fashion Bug for class because it featured Pisa's famous leaning tower.

"What's your daughter do?" Mr. Norman asked, dusting his pie with a blend of provolone and mozzarella, a snowy layer of parmesan. My mouth watered at its acrid scent.

"She's at the college," Arthur said. "Studies Asian countries, religions too, it said in her last letter. She doesn't know I'm here yet."

The college had only twenty-five hundred students. My husband would know her, maybe. I could arrange a reunion. They'd both be grateful, and Arthur would get back on track.

Arthur looked up then, saw me lingering. If he'd been in jail fifteen years, even if they weren't all at a stretch, I wondered when his last time with a woman had been. If he'd grown priestlike in there, celibate, or if there'd been conjugal visits, magazine pictures taped to the wall by his bed.

"Time to pop them in?" he asked, wiping his hands down the length of his apron.

He was proud of his handiwork. Garnering a repertoire so when he got his own place, he could cook for his daughter, make up for whatever he'd missed out on in prison. He wore a long-sleeved polo shirt then, pushed to mid-forearm, and I noticed even through the shirt that his upper arms were small, but sculpted into hard muscles the size of navel oranges. More tattoos covered his neck above and behind the collar of his shirt. One was a woman's name: Lucia.

"Is that your wife's name?" I asked, though I'd only meant to think it.

He followed my gaze and brushed at the spot with his fingers as if trying to rub it away.

"She's more like the reason I don't have a wife anymore, Mrs. M.," he said, curt enough for me to walk away briskly, face burning. We loaded the ovens, and before long the rich scent of cheese and egg and flaky, buttery pastry took up all the space in the room. The students sniffed and smiled, kneaded their knuckles, anxious for a taste.

Later, cleaning up, I apologized. "It's none of my business," I said.

"Don't sweat it," he said. His area was spotless, and still he swabbed the counter with a paper towel as if trying to clean it at a molecular level. "It's all water under the bridge."

I stopped mopping the floor then, gearing up to ask him finally. But he crossed the floor between us swiftly and my mouth snapped closed. I thought he would embrace me then, push me roughly against the smooth plaster wall, or else come at me with a knife concealed in his apron pocket, the very paring knife he'd used to hack apart an avocado on the first day of class. But he only paused in front of me.

"Excuse me, Mrs. M," he said, tossing his paper towel in the trash behind me.

I began mopping again to hide the flush in my cheeks. "Can I give you a ride home?"

He hoisted his backpack and we moved toward the doorway, where I clicked off the lights, plunging both of us into the dim. He dropped one of his hands to the doorknob and held it.

"You have such wild eyes," he said, his free hand kneading the strap of his pack. I couldn't tell if it was just factual, what he was saying, or something else, but my heartbeat picked up and I swallowed with a dry throat. He leaned closer and closed his eyes, then breathed me in. I felt him doing it. My perfume, or just me. I breathed him in too.

"You know, I think I better walk," he said with the flicker of a smile. And then he turned the knob and we both moved out into the dying light of day.

That night I ran a search for flights to Italy. I could fly to Rome for $450. Work my way north through Tuscany to Bologna, Parma, and the Piedmont region, hook east and hit Venice, then back down to Florence. Give myself a month and do it right. But even hosteling, there would be food to pay for, and there I wanted to spare no expense. I bookmarked the page and went into the bedroom, where my husband snored already in bed, his face striated with light.

Week Four

"I wonder sometimes, who was the first person to eat a potato. They're not exactly appetizing raw," Mrs. Norman said. Her pretty voice, like her pretty hands, was flitting and sweet. She seemed fully recovered, yet bigger than ever, as if in the next second she'd boil over.

Both Normans stood slicing their potatoes thin, as I'd told them to, and tossed them into a bowl without any contact of their elbows or hips, maintaining a cushion of air between them.

Arthur had seemed distracted at first, quiet and self-contained, his elbows held close to his sides as if he was trying not to take up space. Still, he spoke up now, producing a smile like a magic trick in his face dotted with constellations of stubble. "It had to be some kind of American. North or South. In the Chiloé archipelago of Chile, they put potatoes in everything. You ever had curanto? They cook it in a hole in the ground. Lots of fish and potatoes. Delicious. Europe didn't even see one until the six-teenth century. Can you imagine the Irish before potatoes? Or the Russians without vodka?" He shivered theatrically as if the very thoughts were death.

"Pardon my asking, but how do you know all that?" Mrs. Norman asked, her voice high as a schoolgirl's. Anyone listening to them went on slicing, but the noise level sunk right down.

Arthur only winked one jaundiced eye and dropped a hand-ful of potato slices into his wok.

I couldn't imagine him in prison. All that surfaced were movie images of men in orange jumpsuits lounging on metal bunks. Kill-ing each other with shanks in the lunch line. Plotting escape in the exercise yard. Pleading innocence. Bragging about their crimes.

The frying stage took longer than I'd planned.

"No, you have to leave them until they're browned," I said, putting all of Mr. Norman's chips back in oil.

"Last week, I'm burning everything. This week everything's supposed to be burnt. No wonder I'm hopeless at this," he said, looking to his wife for rescue.

"Maybe if you'd listen for once," Mrs. Norman said, turning to her right so her back was to her husband, her front to Arthur. But her voice reflected strain, as if she were forcing herself to speak. "I hear you have a daughter. Ours is going to be a girl too."

Arthur went on turning his potato slices in the hot oil. "Her name is Melinda," he said.

"Lily, I need your help over here," said Mr. Norman, indicat-ing the pan where his slices were starting to clump. As he poked at them, a gout of oil sloshed from the pan to the burner, and a tongue of flame shot up. Lily stumbled into Arthur, who had his hands up to catch her before she fell.

It was all over in a flash, but then, as she recovered herself, Lily screamed—an ice-pick-in-the-ear sound. I half expected the juice glasses to shatter on their shelves. As it was, several students raised their hands to their ears.

Arthur released her immediately, then let his hands fall empty to his sides. Lily had clamped one hand over her mouth, and now she stepped backwards, bumping into her husband and flinching when he brought a hand to her shoulder. She turned to him and buried her face in his armpit, her back heaving with sobs.

"I should go," Arthur said, shutting off his burner.

"Arthur, wait," I said, reaching out for his bicep as he passed. The fabric of his polo snagged on one of my fingernails.

"See ya, Mrs. M," he said, pushing past me and out the door, out into the wide world.

In his absence, his potatoes continued to fry toward golden brown.

"We don't know anything about the guy," Mr. Norman argued, his face strained as if someone tugged it from within on a complicated system of ropes. Both hands ran up and down his wife's bare arms as she still heaved against his chest. "Or what he's capable of."

The class was a sea of blank faces.

"Now they're burning," I said, removing his wok from the heat and fishing the crispy rounds out for him with a slotted spoon. Mrs. Norman excused herself, and soon returned with makeup and smile reapplied. She resumed slicing, changing the subject to breast feeding.

After everyone had gone, I swabbed a bleach mixture under each freestanding counter. The mop's saturated gray head encountered some small resistance in the Normans' area: Arthur's backpack, slumped against the rear wall. It smelled of sweat and cigarettes and road dirt and had been repaired often, judging by the paperclip zipper pulls and the swaths of duct tape.

The Best Western was out of my way home, but I swung by there anyway, carrying Arthur's backpack on my hip like a baby. The lobby had a thin beige carpet underfoot and a clerk who watched something with a laugh track on his boxy computer monitor, reaching occasionally into a bag of Cheetos balanced on his lap.

"I have something for one of your guests," I said, transferring the pack to the counter.

The clerk used a long orange-stained finger to click his mouse, silencing the laugh track, then typed Arthur's full name in slow, hesitant keystrokes. I watched his gaze jitter over the results on his screen. "Room 322," the clerk said, yawning. "Want to leave it for him?"

The elevator made a singsong chiming, and I turned to face it. "No, thanks," I said, remembering Arthur's hands on Mrs. Norman's white arms. The way his touch had scared her.

Aerosmith played in the elevator, a blast from my husband's childhood, tinny in the small mirrored space. My husband would be getting hungry by now. I could see him in his armchair, scanning the evening news and listening for the sound of my car in the driveway. In our early days we'd gone skiing in the Berkshires, hiking, camping; we'd traveled to Vermont or New Hampshire or Pennsylvania for concerts on a moment's notice. He'd sing to me, his voice high and pitch perfect, and we'd make love on a blanket in our backyard. These last few years, though, he'd stopped wanting adventures, except the one I wasn't ready for.

He was satiated with experience, and I was endlessly hungry, a bottomless pit.

The third floor was deadly quiet. Arthur's bag weighed on my hip like an actual child, one grown too heavy to be carried around. It was a smoking floor, and the ceilings had yellowed over; the carpets were losing their red. I had an urge to cover the peephole with my hand before I knocked.

"Arthur," I said, rapping softly. I expected to wait a minute or so while he roused himself from the bed or a chair, stubbing out a cigarette on the way over. I'd never seen him smoke, and it made him seem more romantic somehow, a Marlon Brando on the other side of the door. A poor, put-upon James Dean type, misunderstood by the world. Maybe he'd been wrongly convicted of whatever it had been. Maybe he was really an innocent man.

The door swung open almost before I'd finished knocking, but his face—open and inviting before he saw me—arranged itself into a mask of politeness. "Mrs. M," he said. "Won't you come in," as if I'd arrived just in time for tea. "I thought you were someone else," he went on, though he seemed absolutely unsurprised to see me.

I'd expected tube socks flung everywhere, clothes draped over chairs and surfaces, an unmade bed. And I'd expected him to have stripped to a wifebeater and jeans, feet bare, hair rumpled from sleep. But he wore the blue polo shirt and Nikes he'd worn to class, and his room didn't look occupied. A closed suitcase stood off to the side, and every surface was clear, from the dresser to the bathroom counter to the bed with its hospital corners. It seemed he'd only skimmed the surface of this place, never intending to stay. The scent in the air was of lemon air freshener. I spotted the can on his bedside table beside a newspaper, the same one my husband read daily, which was neatly folded along its original lines.

"Your bag," I said, holding it out with two hands.

"Much obliged," he said, taking it from me and setting it next to the suitcase. There was no place to sit but the bed, so he sat on one side, creasing the flowered comforter, and I perched sideways on the other.

This hotel room was made for encounters like this one, and had seen stranger couples than us. I hated to think about what might be living microscopically on the comforter.

"I'm sorry about today," I said. There was a good three feet of space between us, as if we'd left room for both my husband and Lucia, whoever she might be.

He waved the incident away as if it were a fly. "Don't blame her. For all she knows, I went away for rape." He looked at me then, full in the face, leaning slightly over his straight arm, a blue vein pulsing and pulsing through his inked bulldog.

"You didn't, though," I said, feeling confident now, feeling I had him figured out.

He fiddled with the bottom hem of his shirt, staring down intently. "I didn't," he said.

I wasn't going to get a better window to ask him than this one, but he looked so private, sitting there. So remorseful. I picked at a plastic thread in the bedspread that had come loose.

"You didn't have to bring me my bag," he said. "It's just crap in there anyway. Just contingency plans." He leaned back on an elbow and brought his legs up onto the bed.

I curled my own legs up so the two of us were on an island. I wished I'd finished his chips and brought them to him now. We could have fed them to each other, crispy and salty and greasy between our fingers and tongues and teeth.

"It was unfair, what Lily did," I said. "I wanted to make sure you were okay."

He cocked an elbow behind his head and lay back into the bed. "You're a beautiful woman. Don't get me wrong," he said. "But I know what I look like, so what I'm wondering is what's so wrong with your life that you're here with a fuck-up like me."

"What about your daughter? Does she think you're a fuck-up too?" I felt braver now, sitting higher than him on the bed, the door closed but unlatched behind me.

"She's smart. She stays away," he said. "I got some pretty bad habits. They left me in a pretty bad way." He held out an arm across the bed, and I thought he was reaching for me, so I took his hand, turning the willing victim. Our palms dragged against each other with a thin lubrication of sweat, and I felt my heartbeat spike. The country of infidelity was one I'd never thought to visit, a place with no taste—only texture and temperature, pure sensation.

He held his arm stiffly, though, curling his fingers tight over mine and turning his elbow toward me so I could see the healed-over track marks, scars so many and deep they'd been made permanent more than a decade ago.

"Don't get tangled up with me, Mrs. M," he said, letting my hand hit the comforter.

I stood and darted for the door, though he wasn't pursuing, was barely getting himself to standing. And standing there, breath coming fast in a painful whistle, I felt stupid, cheated somehow. But also free. Freed.

"I'll see you in class?" I asked, an attempt at brightness.

"Sure thing," he said.

I took the stairs back down to the lobby and stopped at Boston Market on the way home for food to feed my husband, though for once I couldn't imagine eating a bite.

Week Five

It was normal to drop a few students during the course, but this week only half the class showed up. I'd have to freeze the rest of the pork loins and come up with something creative to do with a dozen extra beets. Arthur was one of the missing.

Mrs. Norman was also absent, and Mr. Norman set about his preparations as if readying for war. While his pork loin simmered, he dashed an onion into a thousand tiny pieces and peeled and chopped beets until his fingers were stained the deep crimson of blood. He kept swiping his hands across his apron, drawing red streaks against the black and white.

At the end of class, Mr. Norman asked for extra Tupperware. "The wife is staying with her mother a few days," he said. "Pre-baby jitters."

His borscht smelled rich and delicious, and when I inserted a wooden spoon in the center of the pot, so many vegetables were crowded in there that it stuck straight up: the sign of a very good batch. I helped him split it into two separate containers.

"You're starting to get it," I said. It was hard to stay angry at a good cook.

"Do you have kids?" he asked, tightening the lid down on one container and marking it "Lily" with a permanent marker. They'd been married for barely a year, and it would only get harder. I had no wisdom for them.

"I'm not cut out for motherhood," I said, and felt another burst of freedom.

Even though we'd parted awkwardly, I missed Arthur at the front counter, his efficient, nimble fingers peeling the paper jackets off small white onions and working a whisk with brisk, confident strokes. I felt I'd been stood up, as if he'd broken a promise more tangible than his presence in class. I cleaned up quickly afterwards and shut off the test kitchen's lights.

Out in the hallway, a familiar backpack had been dropped by the door.

He'd come after all, without ever intending to stay.

At home, my husband looked up from his Chomsky while on the television a weatherman waved his arms frenetically in front of a giant cartoon rendering of the continental United States dotted with clouds and sun and rain.

"What's that?" he asked, marking his place with a finger still pre-dinner thin.

"A student left it. Want to heat this up?" I handed him my tub of borscht, slung Arthur's bag to the coffee table, and reached for the paperclip-tipped zipper.

"Do you think you should be doing that?" he asked.

I looked up from Arthur's bag, the mystery contents. He'd left it for me, but there'd been no note on the outside, no explanation. "I'm looking for an address," I said. "So I can send it back."

My husband clutched the tub of soup to his chest, face white and slack in the twilight creeping in across the lake. He looked at me that way a minute longer, then slipped like a shadow into the kitchen.

The zipper parted easily. I pushed aside hotel towels and trial-size bottles of Suave two-in-one shampoo and conditioner, feeling like a pickpocket as I fished for a wallet or an address book or a prepaid phone. My fingers landed on something boxy and slick, thick as a textbook. I pulled it out, spilling a pair of boxers and a handful of disposable razors onto the hardwood floor between my feet.

Instead of an atlas or a novel or a dog-eared Bible, I held a paperback *Let's Go* guide to Vietnam.

Vietnam.

I knew they used a lot of noodles and rice, seafood by the coast, and in other places turtle meat and dog. But I couldn't name a single dish. Another country I'd never thought to dream of.

Feeling like a thief, I opened the cover, which was new and stiff. I was looking for an inscription, for the corners of pages to be turned down, for any sign that he'd read it, or that he'd purchased it for me. There was nothing until the pencil scrawl on the inside of the back cover: Melinda's name, her address at the college down the street, and an email.

"Didn't you hear me?" my husband said, emerging from the kitchen with a dish towel threaded through his belt. "It's ready." Outside the window, a seagull skimmed low over the lake, calling out harshly, an ocean bird that had somehow lost its way.

"Thanks, honey," I said, flipping through the thick guidebook, feeling the breeze of its pages on my face. It smelled of glue and laminate.

My husband wiped his hands on the towel, then folded it like a trivet in preparation for our meal.

It was nearly racing season now, and traffic would be humming on the 87 up from the city. I pictured Arthur walking that four-lane highway, but heading north toward Glens Falls and Plattsburgh and Montreal and Quebec where he'd eat candied ginger beef with a side of fiddlehead ferns. Caribou steaks. Fresh venison and sockeye salmon. Saskatoonberries in cream. Sweet beaver tail pastries and custard pie.

He could travel the world again. Go back to those places he'd spoken about. Maybe he would. He was a free man. But I too was a free woman, and here I was, right where I'd begun.

Maybe some cages were harder to shrug off than others. Maybe he hadn't headed north.

Through the windows open to the lake, the birds struck up a chorus now, those seasoned travelers. On the television, the weatherman had given way to local news.

"I'm not very hungry tonight," I said, closing the book. My husband held his hand out for the book, then took a seat in his armchair to thumb through it.

He flipped the pages more slowly than I had, his plump face sober and pasty, like dough. I watched him puzzle out the complicated city names, heard him whisper their syllables like the mystic words of some ancient incantation. Then he closed the book softly.

"What happened to our five-year plan?" he asked.

I knelt between him and the television, which droned of accidents on the highway, a small fire started and snuffed in an abandoned home. He wore a pair of old cords soft from many washings, and I ran my thumbnails down between the worn ribs.

"I'm not ready," I said. "I want to see the world first."

He let his head drop and slid the guide toward me down the length of his thigh.

"Then that's what you should do," he said.

He had his wedding ring off for dinner, so I went to the kitchen to dish out the borscht, though I knew he'd prefer something simpler, something more American, something to his taste.

Week Six

She was still in town for a summer program. Melinda Brown,

95

daughter of Arthur, Asian Studies major, journalism minor. I asked her to meet me before my last class, explaining that I had something that belonged to her. Best case scenario: Arthur returned for his backpack and Melinda arrived in the same moment. Joyous reunion ensued.

In truth, I didn't expect her to show. But I was alone in the test kitchen, prepping the counters with bowls and spoons and ingredients for Bobo Cha Cha, when she stepped gingerly in through the door, big sunny curls bobbing with every step and a purse gripped white-knuckle-tight on her shoulder.

She was fair and unlined. I saw nothing of Arthur in her.

"Melinda," she said, with a wary hand held out to be shaken.

I didn't know how to begin. "Your father wanted you to have this, I think." I handed her the *Let's Go* guide, waited for her face to break and crumple.

"I already told him I don't want it. Twice," she said, thrusting it back without ceremony. "I don't want anything from him."

I felt betrayed somehow, as if he should have told me he'd already been to see her.

"What about his belongings?" I toed the backpack, which sat at my feet like the last kid at summer camp waiting to be picked up.

"Burn them," she said, lifting solid, swimmer's shoulders in a rough shrug. "You know what he's done, right? What he's like? Do you know who you're helping?"

At first, of course, I'd wanted to know, like everyone, what Arthur's crimes had been. I couldn't imagine that he'd amassed his fifteen years on the inside just for being a heroin addict. But I distinctly didn't want to know now. I just wanted to pass the last of him on to the last person likely to care. But now I knew there was no such person.

"Maybe he'll come back for it," I said. "If he's not back in Mexico yet."

"You must be kidding," she said, already edging out of the

room. "He's never left the States—hardly even left this one—except where the army sent him. But I hope you're right about Mexico, and I hope he stays down there."

She turned to leave, heels clicking brightly toward the door.

"Are you studying Asia in school because he served in Vietnam?" I asked. "Isn't that what you said in your letters?"

"He said I wrote to him?" She stopped and hung her head on her neck, shaking it slightly. "Never mind. I don't want to know what he said. But Vietnam's no excuse," she said. "PTSD or not." She turned around to face me and I saw her eyes had gone shiny. "There's no excuse for some things."

When she turned to go this time, I let her, but I stored Arthur's backpack in the supply closet. Just in case. The *Let's Go* guide I kept.

And this week only one counter was empty.

I like to think Mrs. Norman woke before dawn and reached over to shake awake her Mister. He carried her bag to the car and secured the belt over her stomach. It was dark, but they didn't have far to drive, as her contractions spun out faster and faster.

While I led my students in peeling sweet potatoes and rinsing off handfuls of screwpine leaves, Mrs. Norman sweated and swore and sucked on ice chips, crushing them between her teeth and letting the shards melt on her half-frozen tongue.

I knew how that ice would dissolve slowly, wetting her throat but tasting of nothing.

Bitter, Sweet, Salt

Games

When I get home from school, Steven's friends have spread themselves like afghans over couches and recliners and the living room's
rose-print rug. I feel the press of them even before I get to the
arched doorway, and know they will be sipping at cans of Coke
and killing each other with video games. They will be talking
about the Red Sox's chances, and about girls, pretty ones like Tina
Carbine and Melissa Gray, juniors at their high school they want
to screw or already have.

"Hey, Cheryl," says Steve, my brother—a good guy almost all
the time. He shoves Matt off the loveseat to make a space for me
and flicks his hair, the color of marsh grass, a sunburned straw,
out of his face. When we were little, we'd pretend to be twins, and
people would believe us.

I kick off brown clogs and tuck my legs under the school skirt
that's blue plaid and itchy on bare skin. The room changes with
me in it. There's a cloud that settles or lifts. It's hard to tell which.

Curly-headed Matthew's on the floor, sitting close enough so
I hear his thick breath. There's Greg, facing the TV, a controller in
his hands. There's Paul with reddish hair and the other controller,
in an easy pose on the sofa, legs kicked out and open, feet splayed
wide apart, big feet in dark blue Nikes. There's Paul.

Greg jams his thumb down on a red button and Paul's fighter flies back against a brick wall.

"Where's Martha?" I ask, looking around. She usually tackles me at the door with a new crayon scrawl, something bright and messy and alive. In the fall she'll start kindergarten at St. Bernadette's already able to read. She can't wait for the uniform and likes to parade around in my extra skirt, hem dragging on the floor. She is so eager to grow up.

"Doctor," Steven says, flipping through a *Sports Illustrated.* "Another earache."

Next year I will leave St. Bernadette's for the town high school where Steven will be a senior. I'll put away my uniform and wear sweatshirts with the school colors, purple and white, and cheer for the Canalmen, and behind the equipment shed I'll pregame with purloined cans of Busch beer from my brother's stash and then file into the bleachers with my friends Lauren and Alex and Ingrid to huddle under woolen blankets, warm with popularity and our cold cans of bootleg beer.

Outside the day is crystal. The glass bird feeder hanging on a pole in the backyard throws refracted light that catches on objects in the living room, playing blue and green over Matt's dark brown curls, coloring white floor tiles pinky orange red. There is the green backyard stretching to the tree line, the rusty swing set, the beach close by but out of sight.

"Is Lauren coming over?" Steven stretches and flips a page in his magazine. I see a full-page spread with a trio of Red Sox players standing by each other, clearly posed. There's Roger Clemens, Mo Vaughn, Jason Varitek. It's early May easing toward June and only the beginning of the new season's long, slow heartbreak.

Steven is in love with Lauren, my best friend, or thinks he is. He dreams about her in English class while students all around him tuck hunks of Juicy Fruit into cheeks to read parts aloud from *Romeo and Juliet.* When she comes over, he drops things, bothers us, plays his music loud, talks on the phone where we can hear. She is thirteen, like me, looks older, and I know what he's getting at. It's May and he has no date for the Junior Prom. He turns a page, and when it settles I turn away from the grunting battle on the screen. "Maybe," I say. "Maybe not. What do you care?"

He rolls his eyes.

I pretzel my legs and take a couch pillow on my lap. Matt drags dark sluggish eyes over my bare knees. Outside, sassafras leaves roil in the sea breeze, flashing veined undersides like palms held up in supplication. Paul lets out a howl of defeat as Greg's avatar sends him flying from the ring and drops his controller on a cushion. He hangs his head back on his neck, and I memorize the shape of his Adam's apple. He's lived up the street as far back as I remember. Drinks on weekends when his parents leave town. Wears T-shirts under plaid shirts. Loose jeans hanging from square hips. Cologne.

"I'm off," Paul says. "Like a prom dress." He winks at Matthew taking up the second controller. He winks at Steven next to me, then stands and stretches in a chorus of crackles and pops, finally loping in front of me to rip the pillow from my lap. His hands against the print of purple flowers are calloused and hard and smooth from hours of pounding Steven's old basketball in the driveway. Two on two.

Paul's prom date is on the field hockey team. She wears jewels with angular cuts, emerald earrings on any old weekday. Makeup and kitten heels, except on the field where her cleats bite the grass. Dana's a year older than Paul. On a recommendation from one of my father's friends she babysat for me one time, years ago. We had a Barbie fashion show before she put me to bed and took up the phone, whispering to someone not-Paul everything she'd do to him as soon as she got off.

"Cher-Bear, when'd you get here?" Paul asks, kneading the pillow. "Didn't notice you come in."

It's a lie I could drown in and die happy, but I won't crack.

"Really? I noticed you get your ass kicked," I say, head buzzing, full and on fire.

This is what it's like to be thirteen: everything is electric, every surface a conductor.

Paul's redheaded, pale behind a fine spray of freckles. Standing over me, he is impossibly tall.

Steven looks between us, brow drawn like he's missed a joke. "Where you off to, man?"

"Got a date," Paul says, kneading the pillow. Something stings, and it takes a minute to know it's my own finger in my own mouth where I've bitten a pinky nail to the quick. Paul watches me pretend not to watch him. "Gotta fly," he says, "gotta run." He tosses the pillow up and catches it.

We used to play catch in the empty lot next to my house. It doesn't belong to us, but the neighbors never complained. It happens less now that everyone's older. We'd toss baseballs around, or a Nerf football, me and my brother, Paul and his brother Jake, who's gone now to college. We'd meet up in the empty lot on summer nights, and I started loving Paul before I could put a name to the way the way he stood out from the background like a planet does in a sky full of stars.

He tosses the pillow up one more time and lets it fall into my lap. "Hey, Cherry," he says to me, an old nickname, one he knows I hate. He's walking toward the arched door, making his exit, and when he's sure I'm watching he reaches behind his back and lifts his plaid shirt above his waist—smooth line of blue elastic marking the top of his boxers—then extends both middle fingers and inserts them into both back pockets. "Notice this," he says.

Socialized

St. Bernadette's is the only Catholic K–8 on the upper Cape, and my class comprises the whole of the eighth grade. We don't have dances, but one Friday a month the nuns throw us socials, which are basically dances with preapproved music, board games, and heavy supervision.

After lunch on a Friday halfway through May, grades 5 through 8 march into the gym in orderly lines clad in blue plaid and white shirts. The boys wear crisp collars and ties. Lauren walks behind me in line and hums something by the newest boy band.

Her hair is down today, long and curly to her waist. My mother once told her she looked like Venus sprung from her clam-shell, then showed us a picture in a leather-bound book. I could see it, but Lauren got mad. She's skinnier than Venus, it's true. Later I asked what beauty I looked like, but my sister was crying for a hot water bottle, so my mother never answered. Martha's ears can get very bad.

In the gym someone set up the long conference tables we eat lunch on and arranged a semicircle of folding chairs around a CD player. The boys put on fast songs first. Will Smith, who we can play because he doesn't swear. Sugar Ray. Someone's Salt-N-Pepa because Sister Maude is napping in a chair against the wall. Three little kids start playing Yahtzee, and I see three more toting Life.

Candyland was my favorite at Martha's age. I remember rounding the corner into my father's office, where he'd hold up his hand to mean "Not now, pumpkin." He's a land surveyor, and maps plaster his office, topographical and aerial and regional, inter-mixed with pinned-up Polaroids of houses and forest and squat cement boundary markers. I used to go with him, sometimes, to scout out property lines. We were explorers whose job was to make the unknown known.

In the chair next to me, Lauren crosses her legs right over left. She passes me a piece of forbidden Trident, and we chew surreptitiously.

"Who do you want to dance with?" she asks, bouncing her hanging foot.

"No one here." We giggle behind hands with nails painted the same shade of medicinal pink.

Lauren switches her crossed leg. "Alex is all right," she says, nodding to the makeshift stage where he stands nodding behind the CD player like a real deejay. He's got bony shoulders and slim, barely-there hips, floppy blond hair that lifts and resettles on his head like sticky strands of cornsilk.

"I guess," I say.

Behind us two little girls drop a game of Sorry!, and we hear the pinging of place markers on the polished gym floor. They stoop to gather the pieces. One has twin French braids, the other a straight brown bob. Lauren and I half-turn in our chairs, eyebrows raised, and their eyes get big; their hands hurry to rectify the mess.

Alex pops in a Boyz II Men album, starts with "End of the Road," slow and sultry. Lauren and I switch our crossed legs and look anywhere but at the milling group of boys. Travis and Jenna stagger our way, her hands arm's-reach on his shoulders, his grazing her sweatered sides.

Ingrid Berry and her perm bounce across the room. She reaches for Robert. "Come on," she says, and he does. There are titters from the scattered pairs of sitting girls, but even though I am laughing too, I think she is brave. I think of Paul in his front yard, mowing. He'd let the motor die when he saw me coming. "Hey," he'd say, hanging his headphones around his neck. Sweat, cologne, new-mown grass. I'd cross the lawn, leaving footprints. Reach for him. "Come on," I'd say. And he would.

Alex appears in front of us, nods to me, nods to Lauren. The song is half over, but the next song will be slow too. It takes that long for the couples to get situated. "Hey, Cheryl," he says to me.

"Hey."

He turns to Lauren. "Wanna?"

They move sideways, grapevine stepping, to the middle of the dance floor. His hands almost get around to her back. Her hands lace at the back of his neck. This is as close as we are allowed to get. Any closer and one of the nuns, Sister Barb, Sister Maude, will separate the couple with two wiry strong hands. "Leave room for Jesus," they'll say.

I stand up to get a lollipop from a bowl by the door when there's a tap on my shoulder. Sean Tran wiggles his eyebrows up and down until I laugh and follow him to the dance floor. He's tall for thirteen, skinny, with hair as black as the ocean at night. I've heard him speak Vietnamese on the lobby phone, and the words flowed out of his mouth as smooth and pretty as a ribbon.

Because he's so tall, only my fingertips make it to his shoulders. We sway to a cover of "Yesterday," and the gum on his breath wafts strawberry between us. After a minute he spins me, dips me, dances goofy with straight legs kicking front and back. I'm laughing too hard to thank him when the song ends, but he's already back across the room calling, "See you on the flip side."

One-on-One

After the social, Lauren comes over with an extra bag for staying the night. The boys are in the driveway, shooting hoops and talking smack. Lauren's walk slows down a tick, seeing them, but not because she's afraid.

"Think fast," Steve says, making like he's going to whip the ball at my head. It's a fake, and his other hand comes up to stop the ball.

"Dickhead," I say, without heat.

Next to me, Lauren gives a little screech, then cups her hand to her mouth. "Shit," she says, and grins at me. Steven stands evenly on both feet, facing us, passing the ball from one hand to the other. Lauren opens her mouth like she's going to say something, then closes it. Steven grins with one side of his mouth.

The door next to the garage swings open for Paul to come out with a bottle of orange Gatorade, plaid shirt knotted around his waist and pulling tight his faded U2 T-shirt. Matt follows him out.

"Hey, Cherry," Paul says. "Hey, Cherry's friend."

Lauren's still staring at Steven, mouth slightly open, as if she can find neither a reason to keep looking nor one to look away. Paul darts between Lauren and Steven and steals the ball out of Steve's still hands. He dribbles one-handed, splashing orange from his bottle, slicking the asphalt shiny.

"Watch it," I say, backing away from the spray.

"Yes, ma'am," Paul says, tossing back the rest of his drink. He throws the bottle to the side of the drive where mint grows in the summertime. "I'll get that later," he says. He backs up, dribbling faster, lower to the ground, eyes steady on mine. "Come on," he says. "You scared?"

Behind him, Greg and Matt give up on ever getting the ball back. They go in through the door next to the garage and shut it behind them. My mother's car is parked on the street, so she must be inside, and Martha too. I wonder if she's feeling better.

"You so would have," Lauren says from far away, and I see that she and Steven are standing off to the side of the basket that's screwed onto the wall over the garage. She's got her arms across her chest, holding her elbows. His sloppy grin makes his cheeks round out like doorknobs, and a pit yawns in my middle seeing it. *She's not for you,* I want to tell him. We are still in our school skirts, Lauren and I. Fresh from the social that was not a dance.

Paul dribbles and pouts. "You're really going to leave me hanging?" He dribbles closer, right up to the tips of my clogs. He breathes sweet citrus and I think of hard candies, lollipops, ice cubes, something that would crack between my teeth and splinter. Between us the ball beats like a heart.

"Fine. To ten," I say, dropping my bag and walking forward so he has to dribble back. By the garage, Lauren winds a curl around her fingers and Steven digs hands deep in his pockets. The pit of my stomach fills with a thick, greasy weight.

Paul bounce-passes me the ball. "Check," he says.

I pass it back, then move up to block, arms out to the sides, knees bent, scuttling like a crab as he bumps me closer to the basket, a warm body shoving up against mine. With every step my skirt swishes close to revelation.

He fakes a shot and I jump to block it, shirt pulling out of my skirt, air brushing my stomach in a quick kiss. When I am down, he jumps up for real; shoots, scores.

"Two points to the master," he says.

"Pearl Jam?" Steve says from behind me. "It's a bootleg."

Then Lauren: "Love to."

I'm dribbling to the drawn chalk line marking half-court, and when I turn to check the ball, Steve has opened the door for Lauren. All around me gears are turning; all around me events will take their course. Lightning cracks in my middle. Something's about to happen that will be out of my control, or even worse, within it. But for now it's me and Paul in the tar-smelling driveway, me sweating in the asphalt's stored heat from the sun.

I feel dampness at my hairline, and the afternoon stretches out, on and off sunny, and a little cool, late-May Cape Cod beautiful. This game will not be cut short by light.

I pass the ball to Paul, who's standing up straight, no smile. "Check," I say. He passes it back.

He's a full foot taller than me, looming, one arm low for balance, one arm following the ball like a compass needle finding north. I dig at him with my shoulder. His shirt smells of Downy, but the skin underneath is all salt, all earth. We move together. He slips in a Gatorade puddle, and I take the layup. "Two to two," I say, this shared solitude like nothing we've done before.

He unties his plaid shirt and tosses it by the Gatorade bottle. "I'll get that later," he says. Grinning crookedly, he asks so low it might as well be a whisper if there's anything I want to take off.

"You wish," I say, knowing for the first time there's the sliver of a chance it's true.

Salt rides the breeze coming in off the ocean with an early whiff of low tide. The rhododendrons in the yard hiss and rattle, and a sudden gust pushes handfuls of my hair into long fingers reaching for his face.

Then he steals the ball, scores again and again. Six to two. I check the ball, and we are both breathing hard, sucking in the breeze, and the sun is slipping away, there-not-there. He eyes the ball as I dribble, eyes my legs behind the ball where they blur against the hardtop. One hand wards him off, the other pounds the ball between earth and sky, earth to sky, as we both move toward the basket. When he stops sliding, my hand comes to rest on the U in U2, pushing at first, both of us laughing at what would be a foul in a real game. The ball still pings from my hand against asphalt.

Against his shirt, my hand is a ghost, and his chest is hard and damp. He's not trying to block me anymore, not doing anything but watching my face and feeling my hand on his heart. The longer it stays, the warmer he gets, so I can feel the skin, the muscles behind the skin, the lungs moving his chest in and out, pushing my hand back and forth. He's just a boy with a body like other boys.

One of his hands comes up over my hand flat on his chest, sandwiches it there. It's not warm now but hot, and not just under but over. We are sweaty and close and moving like the bellows in some huge machine. There are his eyes, finding mine, there is his red hair, there are the pickup games in the field and all the girls he loved or pretended to before my eyes. Here is my hand on his heart.

"Your move," he says softly, a dare and also just the truth.

I tear free, stumbling back, and the air is sharp in my throat. He's still, watching me, and when I put up a basket—swish, no rim—he doesn't try to stop me. Six to four.

His eyes are slits. He checks the ball. "Steven's going to do your friend," he says. *Do*, he said, punched the *∂*. Dribbling into me. His face so hard and cold I wonder that he can ever make it smile.

"My mother's home," I say. "My father will be soon." As if that is all that is needed to prevent a tragedy. At the social, Lauren had looked only at Alex on the dance floor. And Steven wouldn't. They are watching Greg and Matt kill each other with Kung-fu. She is sitting with her hand on his chest.

I raise my hand and block his hook, the ball bouncing toward the street. I chase it, coming back with it fast. Paul lingers by the basket, waiting to pounce. I stop short and put up a jumper that falls neatly through.

"Steven wouldn't," I say, and watch Paul make that face smile, crack the deep lines.

And I know Steven's just a boy, another boy with a body like other boys. He might.

Inside, my mother plays Candyland with Martha in the dining room, taking up the whole table. In the living room, sprawled on purple flowers, Greg and Matt beat out each other's brains across brick walls. The pain is all virtual. In my brother's bedroom Eddie Vedder wails on boom box. He's cleared off a spot on his bed.

"Don't you want to rescue her?" Paul checks the ball, brings it up to meet me. Inside he is laughing. He thinks I believe in rescue.

"Why would I want to?" I ask.

He shrugs and fakes left, dribbles for a clear shot, and puts it up without using the backboard. He could shoot over me anytime, he is that tall.

I check the ball. He's up by two and two away from the win, but he's been winning the whole time anyway. He's been winning my whole life.

"Doesn't it piss you off that she'll go to the prom without you?" His lips twist in something like pity, and I can see it. Packed limo, slow dancing, Dana on Paul's arm, black silk, under his hands, after party, prom dress comes off like a prom dress.

"She likes someone else," I say, and pray it's true.

The garage door squeals and is slowly swallowed back on its

tracks, revealing the chock-full cave inside where my father pulls in his truck. I park the ball on my hip and stand back to let him pass. I wave with the other hand. "Hi, Daddy."

He looks me up and down, looks at the way I'm breathing hard and sweating through my white shirt in the evening cold with Paul, with Paul, with Paul. I move the basketball in front of my chest. Dad joins us in the driveway, zipping his coat with the sheepskin lining. He's been tramping the woods all day, looking for boundaries and places where boundaries have been breached.

"Nice night," he says, and since the way is clear, he points to the basket. "Go ahead and shoot."

Standing next to each other, he and Paul shake hands as if they were both of them men. I'm at an odd angle, half in the mint patch where it almost becomes lawn. I dribble. The wind's picked up, and now there's not much shelter from the house. I'm getting the breeze right off the water and through the trees, salt and pine sap, but I dribble once and sight the basket, into the wind.

"Drumroll, please," Paul says, hooking thumbs into belt loops. He must be cold without the plaid shirt by my feet, but he'd never admit a weakness.

I think I hear "Yellow Ledbetter" from inside and Lauren's laugh. Paul thinks of Dana. Her contours. The flash of her legs on the field hockey pitch.

The bushes at the corner of the house sound like a spiral-bound notebook lying in front of a fan. I shoot and miss the backboard but catch the rim. The ball falls through, and my father catches it on the second bounce. We're tied at eight now, me and Paul.

"It's getting chilly," Dad says, going back into the garage with the ball under his arm. And just like that, the game is over.

Paul retrieves his shirt and bottle and hands my backpack across the mint. The sun is going down and the wind is picking up. I hold down my skirt with one hand. The inside door clicks as my father lingers a minute, then leaves us out here as if against his will.

"We're locked up," Paul says, jutting his chin at the basket.

"Want to settle it?" Another dare. He's grinning, incapable of growing tired playing the same old game on the same old ground. He's just a boy, I remind myself, and I don't know what else I ever expected him to be.

"Maybe later," I say, and slip on my backpack. He backs up slowly, then faster, jogging back up the street to his house.

Inside, Lauren and Steven are sitting close but not touching on the couch. Greg is kicking Matt's ass with his famous flying roundhouse. Lauren yawns when I flop next to her. "Where have you been?" she asks, thinking *with Paul.* I know just from looking at her that she's still on my side of the line. She thinks the same thing about me.

The Kiss

I wake and hear voices. We've been sleeping in my room, me on my bed under a white comforter dotted with blue hydrangeas, Lauren in a black sleeping bag on the floor. The bag lies empty like a discarded snake skin, gathered into ridges. The voices drift in from the other side of my wall, outside, in the backyard. They are low, hums. I can feel them better than I can hear them.

There's a window in my room, but to raise the shade would scare them away. Them. The owners of the voices.

I slide out from under the comforter. The door is open just to the size of a body squeezing through. In the hall, I note the empty bathroom and, across from my room, Steven's closed door. I press my ear to it, listening hard for legs stirring linen.

Martha's room is next to mine, and she's in there, snuggled into bed with her head on a heating pad. She sleeps on it to help the pain in her ear. Her hair is cut into short copper curls, and spirals stick with sweat to one side of her face. Loose strands flutter in her breath-breeze. Even though she's no longer a baby, they hook up a monitor on nights when Martha's ears are bad. Its light blinks red.

I can hear the voices more clearly now, not through walls but through Martha's cracked window. At first there's a lull, then there is Lauren's laugh cupped in her hand.

"It's a little skunked," Steven says, and Lauren demurs.

"It's fine," she says, like she's a beer connoisseur.

My heart is a jagged fist in my chest. Without seeing, I know how Steven holds his beer cold in his hand, watches moonlight play through brown glass, thinks Budweiser, thinks a girl and the smell of grass and the ocean, thinks she's too young. Knows it.

Martha's a light sleeper. I crouch by the end of her bed, under the window, watching her dream close to the surface of sleep. The baby monitor blinks its red warning every few seconds, and I marvel that my parents haven't yet woken.

Martha whimpers, and her head rolls away from the pad. I freeze between wanting to stay and wanting to flee. In an hour my mother will come trundling down the stairs in her terrycloth robe, switching on lights as she goes. For now it's pink medicine every six hours, but soon, next month or the one after, my sister will have tubes put in. Her forehead creases. She's in pain. She needs this sleep.

Once I've steeled my nerve, I peek over the sill, and even though the two of them are back at the far reaches of the yard, it's easy to see the swing chains saw back and forth. Lauren wears the pair of blue running shorts she went to sleep in, and one of my plain gray sweatshirts. Steven has on his jeans, as if he didn't even pretend to sleep. He's balancing on his swing, sighing through night air, beer planted in the grass to his side. There's a moment when our eyes meet, or I think they do, and I duck down to still my heart.

When I peek again they are swinging back and forth on an alternate rhythm. While I watch, Steven reaches one arm out and catches her chain. It's rusty in his hand, like bark, something not quite solid. She skitters to a halt, and when the kiss comes I'm crying without meaning to. After all, it's not as if it's Paul she's kissing.

Still, she's getting what I know she wanted. And I can't have Paul, or won't. Out the window they are still locked together, and I know what I'm going to do, and how selfish it is.

"Martha," I whisper. There's that queasy feeling back in my stomach. It's the feeling I get when I know something is about to go wrong. I shake her awake until she's moving on her own. It's almost time for another dose of the pink stuff, and my mother would have been getting up soon anyway. My sister raises her voice in pain. It goes into the baby monitor. Upstairs Mom sits up, slowly, with resignation. Her slippers are nearby and she puts them on. There's the slow plod downstairs. I'm back in my room, sitting as close to the window as I dare. Now and then I hear the creak of the swing chains, or the soft chug of beer down a throat.

It only takes a minute and a half of sweating palms and wiping wetness off my face for my mother to register movement in the backyard, for the beer to be discovered, for my father to be summoned, for the tryst to be broken. I stumble into the living room as if the raised voices have woken me up. Martha presses her face into my mother's robe, and that's bad to see, but Steven, when I look at him, is worse. Lauren sits on the couch with her hands in her lap, but Steven stands up beneath the torrent of my mother's disappointment; he shoulders my father's deep voice.

And when I dare to find his eyes, I know how he saw me see them. Why didn't you take her down the beach, I want to say, or into the field? I want it to be his fault. Lauren's curls hide her face. She doesn't suspect, but Steven knows better. For all the love there is between us, for everything that's been good about being his sister, there's some part of him that will always hate that small part of me I already hate myself. There's a part of us that's broken.

Prom

The last Saturday in May, I take the prom picture while a limo idles on the street. There's Greg, impossibly big, bulky in black, smile wide and white as a crescent moon. He's taking Karen Printer. She's wearing strapless teal. There's Matt in a tux and oversize pink polka-dotted tie. When I ask about it, there's too much laughing from the others to make out the answer.

There is Steven with his white boutonnière, blond-brown hair done with gel to look carefully tousled. He's got Melissa Gray next to him in a red halter-top dress, pearls in her ears, a red smile painted on. The guys keep sneaking peeks, and she moves inside her dress like she knows it. Her boyfriend pushed her around in the school parking lot a week before prom. When Steven interceded, the kid gave Steven a black eye and Steven wears that too, like a Boy Scout's badge for bravery.

Lauren and I hang out at her house more, now that it's warmer. We thumb through library copies of famous plays. We are joining the drama club when we get to the high school. Planning to be famous.

Steven looks at me, sometimes, like he can't remember who I am. We shoot hoops in the driveway, and it doesn't occur to him to pass the ball. He'll speak to me if I talk first, but there are no more lazy afternoons on the couch. No more ease. I'm terrified there never will be.

Then there's Paul. He's looking through the camera, trying to see through to my mind. But this is my story, and it only works one way. He thinks he has me figured out. He thinks he would have let me win our last game. He thinks that's what I would have wanted. He thinks I've given up on him. Hopes I haven't. Dana next to him is trim in black, classic lines, a little black handbag, tasteful heels. She's thinking, finally a guy who sees past my boobs. She's hoping they play "End of the Road." She's looking at the camera, smiling big, Paul's warmth at her side, blind to me with my finger on the button, mapping their trajectories, holding their places in time.

The Bounce Back

Maya's new apartment complex had eight units, four to a side across a small courtyard. She'd rented one of them, sight unseen, against her father's advice. The landlady, Alma, was waiting in the parking lot as promised when Maya eased Black Beauty's powerful engine to a stop. The '79 Corvette celebrated the end of her cross-country romp in a musical crunch of gravel. Maya tried not to stare at the woman's sun-spotted shoulders, or the amber folds of flesh melting down her thighs, and climbed into the heat of midday, bending to stretch her legs.

Alma gestured to Maya's car with the business end of her cigarette. "She's a prize."

"Black Beauty," Maya said. "Used to be my dad's. Hell on gas."

Alma grunted, then spun on her heel and began walking while Maya scurried behind. The car had made her stick out on her journey. Whenever she made a pit stop, men dragged their eyes from stem to stern, then looked Maya over the same way. She'd protested when her father insisted that she take it as a college graduation present, but he wouldn't back down. It wasn't her kind of car, she'd said, by which she meant it was too much like him. Flashy. Unreliable. Slick.

"You might be sick of Maine. Sick of me," he'd said the day she left Bar Harbor. "You might think Arizona's got something here doesn't, and it's your right to find out, but this car is all I have to give. You're taking it. End of story." As usual, she gave in rather than fight.

Alma keyed into unit 3. Outside the car, Maya began to realize what it meant to move to a desert in June. She fanned herself with the money order she'd brought for rent. The heat was worse in the apartment. "Call APS for your electric," Alma said, opening the blinds to let a shaft of sunlight onto a carpeted floor. The woman's face shivered with wrinkles. She moved down a short hall to the back door, which opened to a small fenced yard. "Rent's due on the first."

Maya handed over the money. She'd chosen this place for its proximity to the middle school where she'd start teaching in August, and because she had enough savings to swing it until her first paycheck. Her father had hinted at a loan, but she wouldn't ask for money. Taking the car had been hard enough. This place had some furniture, a navy cat-scratched couch, an old cathode ray television, a single bed exactly like the one she'd slept on in her college dorm.

"No smoking, no pets, no funny business," the landlady said. Maya glanced at the cigarette burning between Alma's fingers and the woman laughed. "I own the place, dolly."

Maya followed her back out into the sun. A small fountain, dry, occupied the center of the courtyard. In its shady depths slept a thin black cat with one white paw. Her neighbor to the right had rosemary bushes in woven baskets to either side of the door and a straw welcome mat. In front of unit 2, to the left, a metal lawn chair sat askew next to a coffee can half full of butts. Alma crossed the courtyard to unit 8, where the door bore a sign reading "Office." She paused to drop her nub of a cigarette in the fountain's blue basin. "Get out of here," Alma hissed at the cat, and it leapt out of the fountain, diving beneath the lawn chair's sagging seat.

"Psst, kitty-kitty," Maya said, crouching down. The cat arched its back beneath Maya's hand before winding an infinity sign around her ankles. "Not so fast," she said when it tried to sneak past her into the dim apartment. "No pets allowed."

Inside, sweating in the airless flat, she dug the cell from her purse to tell her father she'd arrived. While it rang, she heard the echo of his goodbye, five days earlier, in their driveway of crushed clamshells. "I hear in some cultures," he'd said, "kids take care of their elders instead of splitting first chance they get. Still, I guess you know your mom would be proud."

"Maybe so," Maya had said. She almost added that he hadn't known what her mother thought while she was alive, so it was doubtful he knew now. But she wanted a clean break untarnished by a last-minute blowup. She had turned twenty-one a month before and was ready to let Maine recede into memory. Within a week her father would meet himself a new squeeze at Archie's and forget to pretend to be lonely. She understood the car was meant to be his vote of confidence for her new job, her new life, but Maya hated the thought of Black Beauty, his bullet-shaped pride and joy, propelling her into all the world she'd yet to see.

When the call went to voice mail, she left a short message, relieved not to have to talk.

Maya knew no one in the city. She called her friends from home and talked until they cut her off. "Heat waves literally shimmer over the roads here," she told her best friend, Anna.

"Crazy," Anna said, and Maya could hear voices in the background. Male and female. "Listen," Anna went on, "we're heading to Old Orchard for the day. Can I call you back?"

Maya called ex-boyfriends and second cousins, describing the sulfur smell rising from her kitchen sink, and her itchy ankles—dry skin, she guessed—and her neighbor-to-the-left's video game marathons and poker tournaments. Midnight in Phoenix was three a.m. for her friends and family, so Maya spent her late nights reading, or watching reruns of *M.A.S.H.* on TV.

On the Fourth of July she sat on her sagging couch listening to her neighbor's blowout slowly become a rager. Just after two a.m., Maya set aside her lesson plan on photosynthesis and stepped onto the back lawn. The fireworks she heard mimicked the cough of her father's motorcycle exploding to life, a sound that usually signaled his departure for another of the "business opportunities" that could take him away for weeks at a time.

"Good one," someone cried. A drunken chorus cackled and shrieked as a few more bottle rockets went off, one landing lit and sputtering in Maya's yellow grass, sprouting a small blaze.

"Shit," she said, running into the house for a bowl of water. The orange licks had spread by the time she got back, and she splashed the fire at its base until it hissed up as smoke. Next door, the music and heavy buzz of conversation seemed to swell. She considered sending the empty bowl, just plastic, over the fence like a Frisbee, but instead rapped on the boards, which stood a foot over her head. "Thanks a lot, jerks," she yelled, flushed and breathing hard.

First the music dropped a notch, and then most of the voices sunk to whispers. "Wha—" she heard, and in the next instant, a head of sandy hair popped over the fence like a jack-in-the-box before disappearing just as quickly. It had clamped a cigarette awkwardly between its lips.

"You set my lawn on fire," she said to the fence.

A chorus of drunken apologies rose up. "Sorry," the same guy said, his head appearing again. Then, "Happy Fourth." Mr. Video Games, she guessed.

"Back at you," she said, throat sour with leftover fear.

She left the firecracker's sodden casing in the center of the yard and went back inside, wondering what her father had done for the Fourth without her there to police him.

All Maya had wanted from him during the four years when cancer flirted with and fed on their family was to help bear her mother's terrible tolerance for suffering, her faith that it served some higher purpose, an idea that turned Maya's otherwise steely stomach. After her mother passed, he tried making up for his absences and flings by working daily at the local Midas, staying home nights to tinker with Black Beauty. But it was too late. Conversations were sparring matches. Her clothes were trashy, her friends losers, her hair too short ("You want people to think you're a dyke?"). His sins made fighting back too easy. In her kinder moments, she knew he was trying—and that he loved her—but those moments were rare. After graduating from college early and on scholarship, she knew it was time to go. Part of her hoped that this time distance would somehow save them.

A week later, a squealing garbage truck dragged Maya from sleep. She tried to place a secondary sound that had worked itself into her dream. Singing. Her neighbor had an Elvis album cranked, and though she could separate his voice from the one on CD, each had its own charm. Her clock read 4:17 and the light was gray. She moved a pillow over her head, then gave in and slipped on her flip-flops. The air outside her front door had a cool taste, foreign to her new Phoenix sensibilities. It was enough to make her cross her arms over the T-shirt she'd slept in.

"The sun'll be up in a minute," her neighbor said from his seat in the lawn chair. A lazy curl of smoke trailed from the cigarette in his hand, and she watched him drag on it before tapping a gray spray over his coffee can. He wore a blue shirt reading Tin Man's Tin Can Diner.

Maya remembered her legs, bare to the thigh, and crouched down on the metal threshold to her apartment, pulling her T-shirt over her knees. She absently scratched at an ankle while the black cat scratched his face against a leg of the lawn chair. "You lit my lawn on fire," she said.

A grin transformed his narrow, freshly shaven face. "How's that for an icebreaker?"

He stroked the cat once and then it padded over to Maya, licking the top of one foot.

"It's a good thing I wasn't asleep," she said. "We all could have burned to death."

"Look around," he said, his smile wide. "This is the desert. We're all on a slow broil anyway." She let an eyebrow lift to show he wasn't off the hook, and he leaned closer in his chair, elbows on his knees. "Hey, I'm just fucking with you. I'm sorry, okay? It won't happen again."

She held out a hand from habit and introduced herself. His grip was firm, warm. "It's nice to finally meet the girl of Maya dreams," he said, not releasing her hand.

Maya instructed her body not to betray her, but a blush rose anyway. "And you are?" she asked.

"Hungry," he said, patting a stomach so flat it was nearly concave.

Maya scratched the black cat's belly. "Well, who's this, then?"

"Mittens—Shithead—what's your pleasure? He's not my cat."

"He looks like an Elvis," Maya said. The animal stretched its limbs, claws emerging.

"You're a fan of the King?"

Maya shrugged. "Not really, but I guess you are."

He brought his face inches from hers. His eyes were pure gray. "What's not to like?"

Maya looked away first, to watch the cat work the tip of its tail with sharp little nips.

"It's been nice chatting, but I've got a date with a time clock," he said, tapping his chest where the Tin Man smiled at no one. "Those old-timers need their flapjacks."

"Don't let me stop you." He was the first person she'd spoken to face-to-face in weeks.

"I wish you would," he said, stretching. "Believe me."

Five minutes later Maya heard a pounding on her door. She pulled on a pair of shorts and swung it open to see unit 2 on the walkway. "My car's dead and I can't be late again."

"You need a jump?" She'd already reached for her keys.

"Actually, it's been dead awhile. Weeks. I just missed the bus I usually take."

"You're asking me to drive you?" There was being neighborly, she thought, and there was taking advantage. Before he could answer, the black cat squiggled through their legs, squirting under the low sofa. The two of them dropped to their knees to try to lure it out.

"If you're going to be late, I can get him out when I get back," Maya said. It was strange to see another person, a man, in her living room, let alone on her floor.

He twisted his thin lips sharply and stood. "He's really not an indoor cat," he said.

Maya had the urge to defend herself. She wasn't looking to keep it, and what would he care if she was? He'd made it clear the animal did not belong to him. But then the cat emerged and began to drag its claws down the ruts in the sofa, and her neighbor scooped it up with one arm. "Good-for-nothing feline," he said, and tossed the creature out the door. Maya got her purse.

"Sweet ride," he said when they stopped by the Corvette.

"I guess." Maya unlocked it. The car smelled of her father: stale cigarettes, spearmint gum, leather. He'd claimed he was getting too old for it. "You'll never be old," she'd told him, and he'd laughed as if it was a compliment. But it wasn't. He'd always be the childish man she'd known when she was herself a child. Her mother had been a dentist, the breadwinner, while he bounced from lawn care to lobstering to fixing cars for friends to "opportunities" that took him away from home whenever things got stressful. If those trips ever made money, Maya had never seen it.

His Corvette couldn't erase the times he'd taken off when her mother was laid out, sweat-drenched, heaving the contents of her stomach into a basin Maya's childish arms could barely span. He'd always return for the bounce-backs, the brief respites from chemo, the hopeful wigs secured on her mother's head for a drive-thru date. Then, when she got bad again, as she always did, he'd hop on his bike and get gone. Nothing on four wheels could change any of that.

"So, where am I going?" Maya said, pulling onto a road all but empty at this hour.

Her neighbor gave her vague directions. The radio blared Phil Collins and he reached for the dial. "No fucking way," he said. "Is that an eight-track? Does it work?"

"Yeah," Maya said. "But I usually use the radio."

"My parents had one in their car. Memory lane, man," he said as he snapped open the glove box and emerged victorious with a tape. The neighbor wore some kind of cologne Maya could barely make out in the car, but it was different and it was good.

"Don't put that in," Maya said. It reminded her more of her father than the car itself.

Her neighbor grinned. "Or what?"

"Or you'll see. It's no Elvis."

He put it in. "The Flight of the Bumblebee" burst out. "What the fuck is this?" He hopped in his seat, putting his hands to the roof so he could beat them there.

"I said you wouldn't like it. It's my dad's," Maya said. "This used to be his car."

"I fucking love it," he said, hooting out the window so his hair swirled around his head.

"You're going to get us pulled over," she said, so busy watching him and the rearview mirror that she nearly stalled at the red light.

"Your pops must be cool," he said, stroking the leather seat like the cat at the complex.

They'd arrived at a silver bullet trailer less train car than UFO. "Is that it?" Maya said.

"Shithole sweet shithole," he said, settling back into his seat. "You're a lifesaver, Maya. Maya hero." He flopped his head to look at her when he said it. She concentrated on parking.

"Original," she said, trying not to be charmed. "Do you have a name, or should I call you Elvis?"

"Works for me," he said, shrugging.

She shook her head, shifting the car into reverse and revving the engine. "Have a good day at work, neighbor," she said. Trailing a hand along the car's curves, he finally got out and crossed to her window, gesturing for her to roll it down.

"I'm Hank," he said. "For real." He picked up her hand, damp and sweaty, from the steering wheel and held it pressed between his two large, dry ones. "And for real, thank you."

He was the kind of guy her father had delighted in warning her about. The kind he claimed to have been, as if all that was in his past. "You're welcome, Hank," she said.

The next morning, Hank must have gotten himself to work. She listened for his throaty singing, but all was silent. In the evening he had one of his poker nights that lasted until dawn.

Staff orientation at J. B. Sutton Middle took up the rest of the week. Maya sat through sessions on Sexual Harassment and Disciplinary Tactics, and attended equipment training on operating desktop computers and focusing overhead projectors. On Friday there was a lunch of cafeteria food, and Maya sat at a table with the other newbies, stirring the buttered corn on her Styrofoam tray and nibbling at the edges of her chicken nuggets.

"It could be my imagination, but I think I can actually smell the hormones in here," said Bill, the prematurely balding math teacher next to her. The first day, he'd cracked jokes all through Rudimentary First Aid until the instructor pretended to send them to the principal.

Maya laughed and lifted a forkful of kernels. "I think that's just *eau de* rancid corn."

They traded student-teaching stories while she ate the cream off her pudding. In Sixth Grade Seminar they received HR paperwork, supplementary assignments to their major teaching areas, and grade books. Maya's area was science, but she'd also been assigned Photography Club.

"I don't even own a camera," she said, laughing on her way with Bill to the parking lot.

He stopped at a pickup truck a few aisles short of Black Beauty and waved his folder. "You think that's bad? Apparently, I'm directing the fall play."

"Must be your star quality," she said.

"T minus ten days," he said, swinging open the truck's door. "Maybe we should get together this weekend, memorize some of these Disciplinary Tactics?"

"Acknowledge, assess, address," Maya said, reciting the Holy Trinity of Happy Classrooms according to the training session. "It's a date."

Hank looked up from a paperback as she approached his lawn chair. "Howdy," he said. He was shirtless, revealing an expanse of golden skin and a bowtie of bronzed chest hair.

"Guess you've been making your bus," she said. Her keys slipped to the walk at his feet.

He scooped them up, handing them over with a grin. "Miracles never cease," he said.

"If you say so." She moved inside where it was cool and quiet, and started fixing a tuna sandwich. When the phone rang, she got it on the third ring, expecting Bill's cheerful voice.

"How's my girl doing?" her father said, his words thinned by distance.

"She's fine, Daddy," she said, spreading mayo on bread.

"She's not doing that hiccup thing on the highway anymore, is she? If you haven't got the oil changed yet, I'll send you a twenty to bring her in."

"I thought it was my car now," she said, knowing the "it" would rankle.

"Me and Val are going to the beach for a few days. I'm telling you like you asked."

"What happened to Jen?" she said, biting into her sandwich and going barefoot out the back door. As if it had been waiting, the black cat trotted past her into the house. On her father's end, metal pinged against metal. She pictured him popping a dent from his new fixer-upper.

"Val's the new receptionist at the shop," he said. "We're taking the bike."

"What happened to Jen?"

"Listen, Magpie, take care of Black Beauty," he said. Maya went back into the cool and peeked through her blinds at the car in the parking lot. It seemed to suck the light from the day.

"Be careful, Dad," she said automatically, hanging up. He'd never had an accident on the bike, but one day he would, according to all the statistics. Her mother had called it the Death Trap.

The cat was on the counter now, navigating the sharp edges of the tuna can with its tongue. "Come here, freeloader," she said, scooping the scruffy cat into her arms and tossing it out front next to Hank.

"You'll be sorry, letting that thing in your place," he said. The cat sat in the dry fountain, a portrait of injured pride.

Maya scratched an ankle, trying to erase her father's voice. "It wasn't really a choice."

"If you say so." Hank marked his place in the book and reached for his pack of cigarettes, lighting up and speaking around the butt. "It's just that Jackson's a regular flea motel."

"Jackson?"

"One white paw like the King of Pop."

Maya stopped scratching her ankle and examined it. Half a dozen red dots ringed her fair skin. She groaned. "Great, I was looking for an excuse to clean all weekend."

Hank ducked inside and came back with two cans of Coors,

handing her one. "He lived in your place with the last girl. She named him."

"Why'd she leave him?" Maya thought of the couch with its ragged striations. She relished the ragged path the cool beer cut down her throat.

"She left in a hurry," he said, studying the can on his knee. She understood then: they'd had something to do with each other. It took a minute for the feeling in her chest cavity to register. She was jealous of a girl she'd never met who'd dated this guy she barely knew.

According to him, the previous tenant broke all of Alma's rules. Kept the cat inside, threw midweek parties. "She'd come knocking on my door looking for a pick-me-up. Total cokehead," he said.

When Maya finished her beer, she broke her own promise to be cautious around him, this sweet-tongued huckster, gray-eyed tease, and went boldly into his apartment. "Hey," he called behind her, filling the doorway, a black shape against the setting sun. A breeze seemed to wash over her damp skin. She'd miscalculated, boxing herself in. Who was he, anyway? As her eyes adjusted to the dim living room, she saw crates in the corners heaped with shrink-wrapped video games and CDs. A dozen of the latest Grand Theft Autos leaned against one wall. Her heartbeat stuttered.

"Grab me one too, okay?" he said before slipping back outside.

Back on the walk, she felt relief to be out in the open. She should keep going back to her apartment, and stay there, she knew. He was a person who dealt in stolen video games and could get a line of coke on a moment's notice. Odds were he was a liar too.

"Do you even have a car?" she asked.

Hank sipped before answering. "Not at present," he said, winking. He must have performed the mechanics of standing, then bending, then scooting next to her, but to Maya it happened instantaneously. Sharing her square of concrete, his body was warm and solid for all his thinness. "You can't blame me for fibbing. How else is a guy like me getting next to you?"

"Liar, liar, pants on fire," she said, the words seeming to issue from someone else's mouth. The sky bled in gashes of red and yellow and violet. "I've never seen sunsets like these."

"Best in the world," Hank said, raising his can to the view.

"Amen," she said, and allowed him to kiss her with his taste of smoke and beer.

Bill called Saturday afternoon. She was on the way home from the vet, where she'd picked up a flea collar and cat shampoo, and was about to head to the Laundromat to wash every item of cloth in her apartment—clothes, bedding, the cushion covers from the sagging couch.

"I thought mini-golf would be fun for tonight, or is that too juvenile?" Bill said.

"To beat the enemy, one must know the enemy," Maya said, and agreed to dinner after.

Talking to Bill, her cheeks grew heated remembering how she'd driven Hank to work only hours before, the two of them rising from his futon before the sun was awake. They'd listened to the radio, and he kissed her cheek before exiting the car. "Fuck this place," he said cheerfully, slinging an apron over his Tin Man shirt. Then he'd thanked her for the ride.

She tried to keep from feeling bad about sleeping with him. She was an adult and single and beholden to no one. Her choices had nothing to do with her father's legacy.

Now Jackson the cat was clean and had been declared a prime feline specimen by the vet, and Maya had a real date with a man who had ambitions, a career, a car. She lugged Jackson in his cat carrier to unit 8 and banged on Alma's door. The woman answered with the chain on, then opened it wider, revealing an interior opaque with smoke.

"I have a cat now," Maya said, holding up Jackson in his carrier as proof.

"Good for you, dolly," Alma said. She held in her hand an ashtray on which a long, thin cigarette burned away, but made no move to drag from it.

"It's going to be an indoor cat," Maya said.

"I figured that's what you meant the first time." Alma took a hand from her door to move it in a circular motion. "Anything else you'd like to get off your chest?"

"No," Maya said, backing across the courtyard. "Just that."

Alma manufactured a smile that barely revealed her teeth and closed the door. Maya heard the chain sliding back into place. Her own apartment smelled of lemon Pledge, and every surface gleamed. She'd run over the whole sofa with a lint brush and shampooed the rug and purchased food and water bowls and a litter box and a whole arsenal of cat toys. "Welcome home again," she told Jackson, releasing him. He took up his accustomed post in the corner of the sofa and set about cleaning himself with great attention to detail.

Hank knocked on her door after work. "Want a brew?" He held up an extra beer.

Maya wore a flared white skirt and pink-striped tank top. Her lips were glossed, her hair blown dry. "Sorry, I have plans tonight," she said, ashamed the second the words left her lips.

"Wow, yeah, I can see that," he said. "Twirl around now. Let me see how you look."

He whistled and she felt a slow heat flood her chest. He retired to his lawn chair and set the extra beer by his feet. "Freedom of choice," he said. "It's a beautiful thing."

This was something her father would do. Take her mother dancing one night, then meet his girlfriend for beers the next. The saliva dried in her mouth.

"I'm sorry," she said, surprised to find she was. The sun was down. Bill was on his way.

"For what?" he said, hackles up. All pride. "I was just looking to kill a few hours."

"We should do something tomorrow," she said, hearing defeat in her own voice.

"I'm not big on plans," he said, "but we'll see. Have yourself a time." She closed the door as he dragged on his cigarette, the cherry brightening like a jalopy's one working taillight.

When Bill knocked, right on time, Jackson took off for the bedroom, skittish in his new-old life as a house cat. "You look stunning," he said. He'd brought a bottle of red, and she set it on the counter, wondering if he meant it for now or later. His monk's tonsure was newly trimmed.

"Well, should we be off?" she asked. The evening ahead suddenly seemed like work. She locked up as Jackson yowled, scared at the way the world had shrunk around him.

Bill turned out to be witty and considerate. They bet the price of dinner on mini-golf and he lost woefully, comically, and got flustered when she accused him of doing it on purpose. In any case, he let her take care of the tip for the Thai food, which was hot enough to bring tears. Back at her complex, he pulled up next to her car and glanced over at it.

"Don't say it," she said.

He turned to look at her. "Say what?"

"Whatever you were going to say. Guys always drool over that thing. It's just a car."

"Yours, I'm guessing." His face showed polite interest. She could tell him the story over a glass of the wine he'd brought. It was the next natural step, but she let the moment pass.

"I have a busy morning," she said. It was mostly true. School started in a week. She still had to plaster her classroom with posters on cell division, the solar system, the scientific method.

"This was nice," he said. Their lips met harmlessly in a stream of cool, conditioned air.

She waited until his taillights faded, then reapplied her lip gloss, ran a hand through her hair, and paused before Hank's door. The nights she'd cursed her father's inconstancy swelled in her head like some nightmare symphony. She'd never understood his ability to smooth-talk every woman but the one he'd married.

They'd taken a family vacation to Colonial Williamsburg once, her mother's last. For two days Maya shared her mother's seat in Black Beauty's belly, and then, while her mother napped at the hotel, Maya's father took her to the restored area, where a blacksmith made her a ring out of a nail. Her father put it in his pocket for safekeeping. Then he left her in the crowd. While a man dressed as a barber from the 1800s waved around a rusty razor as part of his spiel, Maya had looked frantically for her father, panic rising in her throat, a steady heartbeat of *where-did-you-go, where-did-you-go*. She finally found him chatting up a girl in a mobcap a few houses down. The girl had been wearing Maya's nail ring.

Hank opened his door as if he'd been expecting her knock. "Did you kids have fun?" he asked. His television was on to some sitcom, and it made the light strange and shifting.

"I feel like shit," she said.

"Don't sweat it," Hank said, going to the refrigerator for a couple of beers. "It's not like we're engaged." The silver can was so cold it numbed her hand on contact.

She gave it back. "I have some wine next door," she said. "Do you work tomorrow?"

"Fuck that place," he said, pressing her against his kitchen counter. He held her unopened Coors to the small of her back so she arched away from it, into him. When he pressed it to the nape of her neck, she moaned. At her place, she set her bag on the counter and kicked off her heels. He took the corkscrew from her hand and poured Bill's Shiraz into matching yellow mugs.

"Bottoms up," he said, and they clinked porcelain. As they drank, Maya kept recalling portions of her date: Bill tripping at the foot of the windmill, the way his glasses kept sliding down his nose, their chaste kiss in the car. Bill was sweet and smart, a grownup, but Hank was all magnet and around him she shattered into metal filings. It didn't feel in the end like a choice. Her twin bed groaned under their combined weight. She put his hands where she wanted to feel them and cried out when they connected, the two of them falling asleep just before dawn.

The rumble of a revving engine woke her late on Sunday, and she found the half of the bed where Hank had been cool to the touch. Maya fumbled on a T-shirt and a pair of shorts. There was a Starbucks down the street. The stroll would wake her up. She reached into the bowl for her house keys, but they were missing, along with the one for Black Beauty. Outside, the engine growled again, and she pictured Hank goading her awake before speeding off into the sunrise. The pit of her stomach went cold. She didn't even know his last name.

"Shit," she said. Though it was her car now, her first thought was of her father's wrath. Jackson streaked out the door when she stepped barefoot onto the walk, concrete searing her soles. "Shit," she said again, watching the cat sprint into the park across the street.

When she saw Black Beauty still in the lot, her hammering heart began to slow. Hank sat shirtless in the driver's seat, one hand kneading the wheel, elbow cocked out the window. "The Flight of the Bumblebee" issued from the speakers with all its natural lunatic force.

Maya went to his window. "Didn't your mother teach you not to take people's things?"

He looked up, grinning, and turned the sound down. "How about a Sunday drive?"

The hot asphalt beneath her feet made her shift her weight back and forth. "I can't. School starts a week from tomorrow, and I have a lot to get done. Name tags, lesson plans."

His grin only widened. "My pops always said the Lord made Sundays for fishing."

"I had no idea you were religious. Slide over," she said. Her feet were getting crispy. He lifted himself past the gearshift so she could take his spot.

"You been to Sedona yet? Once school starts, you're going to be no fun at all. Come up north with me today and I won't bug you about it again. Scout's honor."

He was right about one thing. She wouldn't have time during the school year. "I'd have to be back tonight," she said, trying to sound stern but thrilling to the bottomless feeling of surrender. "I have a ton of stuff to do at school tomorrow." Plus, she'd promised to meet Bill for lunch.

"I'll have you home by midnight," he said, reaching across the seat to cup her knee.

"Scout's honor?" She ran her hand up his arm glinting with golden hair.

"One day, that's all I'm asking." She helped him pull her past the stick shift and into his lap. "Everyone needs a break sometimes."

Her father had treated every day like Sunday. The tape Hank loved had been a joke before her mother got sick. "You're my honeybee," her mother would tell her father. "You fly away but always come home to your queen."

Maya tore the tape from the deck.

"I have to stop by the diner," Hank said on their way out of town.

Maya laughed. "You're still hungry?" After packing overnight things, just in case, they'd stopped for Grand Slams at Denny's. The way he'd been caressing the steering wheel earlier, she thought he'd want to drive, but he'd chosen the passenger seat.

"I've got some back pay coming. How can I show you the time of your life without the millions I'm due?" He started biting at a ragged thumbnail as she pulled into the Tin Man's lot.

Maya watched him hold the door for an exiting family before she spun the radio's dial, settling on Donna Summer, who'd topped the charts the year Black Beauty was born. She was still singing along to "Hot Stuff" when Hank burst from the diner, taking the steps two at a time.

"Go, go, go," he said, tearing open the door and throwing himself in, shrugging off a string Adidas backpack she hadn't noticed before. She had the idea that if his window had been open, he'd have dived in that way. Before she could ask what was going on, the diner's door shot open and a man took to the steps, enormous gut swaying side to side under his apron, red face screwed up with fury, a shotgun in one hand.

"Hit it, goddamnit," Hank yelled, the first time she'd heard him raise his voice. She screeched out of the lot, watching in the rearview as the cook screamed something after them.

Maya's palms were slick on the wheel. When she started to slow for a yellow light, Hank eased his hand onto her thigh and squeezed gently. "You got it, girl," he purred, and she did not look at him but only stepped on the gas and entered the intersection just as the light turned red.

When they'd gone a few blocks without incident, Hank leaned his head out the window, looking back the way they'd come. "Adios, Vern," he hooted, slapping the roof of the car.

"Was that your boss?" Maya asked. She changed lanes to get on Route 17, but Hank put his hand back on her leg and told her to keep going toward 87 instead.

"Won't that take almost twice as long?" She'd printed directions before leaving, since Black Beauty lacked a GPS.

"What's your hurry?" he asked. "Sometimes the journey *is* the destination."

"You'll have to tell me where to turn, then," she said, watching him stuff the Adidas pack into his overnight duffel. "What happened in there anyway?"

"Vern's a dick about tip-outs. He shorted me, so I resigned." Hank rustled around in the bag, emerging with a cigarette.

"Should I be worried? Is he going to call the cops?" Their get-away, if that's what it had been, was already blurring into a scene from a dream.

"I doubt it," he said, "but maybe we should have mudded up the plate."

Her hands grew cold on the wheel, but when she looked over he was laughing, slapping his knee, ribbing her. She shook her head as they cruised past the red roofs of Phoenix, the mountains almost in sight.

Hank wasn't kidding about savoring the trip. First he made her pull over to ogle the spout of water at the center of Fountain Hills. They were barely clear of Phoenix and there was nothing as far as Maya could see until a stream of water three-hundred feet high punctured the horizon.

"Disgusting, isn't it?" Hank asked, though it wasn't really a question. "In the middle of the desert."

"It had to be a man that dreamed it up," Maya said. She was thinking of her father, though he was no architect. Something about the way the fountain stood out from the nothing sur-rounding them, calling attention to itself, a temporary testament to wealth and abundance that lasted only fifteen minutes at a pop on the hour. As they stood watching, leaning against the hot car, the stream ceased, becoming a one-way waterfall that left the sky thinly blue and empty.

"Daylight's wasting," Hank said, pinching her backside in a way that didn't hurt at all.

They stopped too at Tonto Natural Bridge State Park, view-ing the arch—the largest natural travertine bridge in the world, according to the brass-framed plaque—from a parking lot. Taking in the massive gorge and perforated mountainside, Maya believed it, though she had to look up travertine, which turned out to be a kind of limestone. She liked the bridge, but she liked the heat of Hank's body behind her at the metal fence more, the way his arms seemed to keep her suspended over the drop of nearly two hundred feet as he tasted the sweat that gathered at the nape of her neck.

"How long would it take to hit the bottom?" she wondered aloud. With her body pressed full-out against the wire, her veins hummed, heart thumped, heels lifted from pavement.

Hank's lips buzzed at her neck, then his hands gripped her waist, hoisted, brought her hips in line with the top of the fence. She felt the tug of gravity, an imminent free fall, and yelped, but when he lowered her back to earth there was disappointment woven into her relief. The feeling of flight lived in her limbs still as potential, and she kept seeing herself turning end over end through the air.

There was no privacy at the overlook, but they found a nearby trailhead with a convenient outcropping that shielded them from the main path. She let Hank press her back to cool rock and slide off her top, unbutton her shorts. It was the first time she'd made love outdoors.

Late afternoon saw Maya finally taking the exit to downtown Sedona, which deposited them on a quaint main street of cafes, palm-reading parlors, crystal shops, and signs advertising Pink Jeep Vortex Tours.

"We need gas. Then dinner. I'm starving," she said. It occurred to Maya that she'd succumbed to Hank's designs, arriving late enough to all but rule out a same-day return. But the mountains were beautiful, red striated with brown and yellow, accented by smudges of green mesquite. She'd left a bowl of food outside for Jackson, and the drive back on Route 17 would only take two hours. If they left early tomorrow, she'd be back in plenty of time.

"Pull into that Circle K," Hank said. While she fed Black Beauty, leaning back against her door to take in the view, he went into the store and chatted with the clerk. He jogged back rubbing his hands together. "I've got the perfect place for tonight."

After steaks at the Cowboy Club, where he wouldn't let her see the tab and paid in cash, his directions took them twenty minutes north of the city to a compound of adobe buildings huddled against the rainbowed mountains. She pulled up to the largest one. "This looks pricey."

"Hang tight," he said.

He went in through a large arched door. It was so quiet that she felt bad about the car's rumble and shut it off. The air smelled of lavender and creosote and the possibility of rain, though the sky was clear. The last slants of sun pierced the back window, and Maya was on the point of nodding off when Hank came back with a paper map marked with an X in Sharpie.

Their cabin perched on a cliff overlooking Sedona's cluster of lights capped by the vast desert sky, now rapidly darkening. "This place must cost a fortune," Maya said, dropping her pack in the tiled living room with a dark flatscreen and a corner kitchenette. "Let me pay for half, at least."

"I thought you'd dig it. It's ours till Tuesday," Hank said, taking his bag to the bedroom. Back in the kitchen, he reached into the fridge and liberated a bottle of champagne.

"Tuesday?" She recalculated. If she put in eight-hour days the rest of the week, and rescheduled with Bill, of course, she could make it work. "Let me make a quick call." She went into the bedroom to dial Bill, settling cross-legged on the pillow-heaped bed and shifting Hank's duffel to make room. The top was unzipped, and the Adidas bag within sagged open. A dull gleam of metal caught her eye.

"Hiya," Bill chirped in her ear before she was ready. She swallowed with difficulty.

"Hey, I'm really sorry, but I have to cancel for tomorrow," she said, pinching up thin nylon to see an oily-looking silver revolver nested in a heap of crumpled green bills. She must have squeaked, because Bill's voice jumped an octave.

"Maya? Is everything all right? You sound—odd."

She choked on air before drawing enough breath to manufacture a laugh.

"I'm fine. A friend just came to town unexpectedly. We're up in Sedona."

"Sounds like fun," he said, nothing in his voice but disappointment.

"Would Wednesday work for you?" She pushed Hank's bag to the end of the bed.

"Sure thing. Have a blast up there," he said. She promised to do just that.

She'd known Hank was a thief, though she'd thought a petty one. Still. Maybe she hadn't asked him about the games, or anything else, not even his last name, to keep herself in the dark. No, not maybe. The truth was, she liked who she became around him. Someone daring. Sexy. Impulsive. A loose cannon and, now, a partner in crime.

He'd left the bag open on purpose, she thought. He wanted her to see, and make a choice.

"Maya, are you coming?" Hank was whistling out there. A pretty tune she didn't know.

"Just a sec." The person she really wanted to talk to was her father. He'd know what to do. She brought up his number on her phone. Of course, he'd also be the first to say he told her so about Arizona, and guys like Hank, and that running never fixed anything—he should know.

"Any bubbly left?" she asked, joining Hank on the sofa. He hadn't turned on any lights. Over the TV, which held their dim reflections, she saw he was staring out a long, narrow window framing a panorama of pristine night sky. He handed her a flute and filled it.

"This is a country of wonders, and I bet you haven't seen the half of it." His arm came around her shoulders. She caught herself stiffening, but made herself give in to his warmth.

"I've seen a few things," she said. The champagne's bubbles burned her tongue.

"Vegas is a day's drive. That would be fun with money to burn." If he was joking, nothing in his voice let on. She knew what she was supposed to say. She had a life waiting for her in Phoenix. A job. A sweet boyfriend, if he forgave her lie. A half-wild cat, and a father somewhere who would worry.

"We can't take Black Beauty. You said it yourself. Vern saw the plate." She waited for him to deny, or explode. For his true self to surface. Or maybe her own. She'd kept driving, after all, when she knew everything about him that mattered. She was already an accomplice. Or whatever it was called, an accessory after the fact.

Hank stopped studying the Milky Way. In the dark, his face was a blank. "It's cherry," he said. "Easy to sell. I know someone in Flagstaff who could help us."

Maya set down her flute and went to the window. "Who are you, anyway?"

He downed his champagne in a swallow. "I'm pretty sure you know by now."

"So did your last neighbor, I guess."

In the glass, Sedona's stars shone below, the Milky Way above. Wonders upon wonders.

"Look, if you want to go back, we'll go. No problem. Or, we can go forward. Vegas. Hollywood. Mexico. There," he said, and came to the window to point at the fingernail moon.

After all those years of her father tearing out of the driveway and returning unscathed, she'd hated him in the end not for leaving but for leaving her behind with a woman whose needs were endless and exhausting, whose pain Maya couldn't hope to slake. She'd despised her mother's beatific endurance by the end almost as much as her father's vacillation. It had taught her that sometimes staying could be as bad as leaving. Sometimes it was worse.

"I don't know who you think I am," she said, "but I'm not her."

"I don't know a damn thing about who you were before," he said, trembling next to her, with excitement or fear she couldn't tell. "You can be whoever you want with me."

She pressed a hand to the window. The sky went up and up. "How far is Flagstaff?"

"Close," he said, lips against her ear. "We're practically there already."

She went to the bedroom first, where it was dark and cool. When she closed her eyes, she imagined around them her bland apartment walls, then the sea she'd grown up next to, eating its fill of the granite shore. It was a scientific fact that over time the sea would make those familiar crags unrecognizable. In a hundred years, it would seem a place she'd never been.

Lighter, Bluer, Clearer, Colder

When Brinna wakes, the day is filled with busy grains of snow. Silver light through the curtains turns her whole room frosty and makes the mess stand out, the pile of socks and Barbies by the dresser's feet, the overturned jewelry box, a pair of Raggedy Ann and Andy dolls who lie stretched across the carpet, cloth hands joined by Velcro.

Brinna doesn't like to wake up early and alone on gray mornings like this. The days she likes best are when Daddy comes in to tickle her face with his brown beard. When he pretends not to see the lump of her under the blankets and pats and pats the bed, saying, "Where has Brinna got to? I bet she's up already. I bet she's already shoveled the walk and fed the dog and eaten her breakfast. No need to make pancakes now," he'll say, and only when he stands to leave does she sit up in bed and raise her arms for a hug and say, "I'm only sleeping, Daddy."

And sometimes he has baby Patrick with him in the crook of one arm, and her brother looks at her with those strange blue-diamond eyes. His eyes say that he knows secrets he might tell her someday. Sometimes Daddy can't pat her bed because he's got Patrick in one arm and one hand on Patrick's bottle, which is full of Mama's milk and medicine.

This morning no one comes to wake Brinna. It's a school day, and she hears a commotion downstairs—men's voices and doors slamming—so she swings her legs over the side of her bed. She's in her favorite pair of pink footie pajamas, and her feet make a cool crinkle on the deep blue carpeting. She pushes herself across the rug like an ice skater, hands linked behind her back, and imagines herself in the Olympics, not one of the skaters who dance, Nancy Kerrigan or that other one with the broken shoelace, but a speed skater. Brinna imagines zipping across her room faster than eyes can follow. Her blades are so sharp that anyone in her path would be blown backwards, arms and legs pinwheeling.

Her door is sticky, and Brinna uses two hands to turn the knob. Ever since Patrick came, big breakfasts are only for Sundays. This means Brinna gets to pick out a new cereal every week at the A&P when she goes along with Mama to help carry the bags in. That was how Brinna broke her arm last year, carrying a tall paper bag up the front stairs. She couldn't see over a green fluff of kale and tripped on the last step. They piled into the car, she and Mama in back beside Patrick's car seat and Daddy driving to the hospital while Brinna held tight to her teddy bear, who got his own cast that day too.

In the hall, the commotion is louder. Brinna speed-skates down the hardwood to the top of the stairs. She fell down them once when she was three, but she didn't get hurt, because she is sturdy. Patrick is her opposite, fragile. Now she can hear Mama's voice higher and squeakier than she's ever heard it. Daddy's voice is down there too, along with other voices she doesn't know. Brinna creeps down the stairs one at a time, bumping down on her butt and giggling at each landing. No one has turned on any lamps or anything, and Brinna's skin looks gray in the early morning light. She is a zombie, like the ones in the late movies she watches with Daddy.

Halfway down the stairs, many sets of legs appear in the living room, pacing. Mama's in a long blue skirt and Daddy's in soft brown corduroy. The other legs are blue and crisp with ironed edges. She bumps down farther. Patrick lies still on a long bed with metal legs.

This has happened before. In kindergarten, Brinna once brought her mother and Patrick for show-and-tell. "My brother has five rooms in his heart instead of four," she'd said while the kids watching nibbled their glue sticks and blinked. The teacher nodded her on. "He's going to have an operation," Brinna said, and she'd pictured the way it would be, like the game she was good at, tweezing a plastic bone out of a man's body without making his nose light up. Patrick's doctor would fix the problem, then sew his tiny chest with a silver needle as sharp as a speed skater's blade. Her mother wrote the words "Tetralogy of Fallot" on the blackboard along with the day's other show-and-tell words, "bullfrog" and "bird's nest" and "piccolo," then took Brinna out of school early, since she'd only come to get her on their way to one of Patrick's appointments. It saved her a second trip.

All at once the commotion moves into the hall and out the door at the bottom of the stairs. The matching men push and pull the bed out the door, Mama stands in the door, and Daddy has her two hands in his and they are squeezing so the skin is white and their faces are tight and white like the light coming in from the open door along with hard pieces of snow. Daddy is reaching for Mama's parka from the front hall closet and kissing her cheek and saying, "Go, just go," and Mama doesn't even see Brinna even though Brinna has bumped all the way down. The door closes and Daddy turns around. "Hey you," he says. "Good morning."

The road to Nana's house is slick and twisty, and once the car makes a sharp jerk to the left side and then to the right. Brinna wears a hat with a pom-pom on top. She feels like a gopher in her ski jacket, bundled up inside a cozy, warm den.

"It's a snow day," Daddy says. "So you're not missing out on school."

"How many inches are we getting?" she asks with her nose to her backseat window. She's still too short to sit up front.

Her father looks into the rearview, and Brinna sees his eyes are red. "It should stop by lunchtime," he says. "Definitely by dinner, and your mother and I will be back by then."

At Nana and Grandpa's house Brinna will get to bring an assortment of kitchen utensils outside to the back slope. Her grandparents live in a small neighborhood of houses called Hideaway Village. In the summer, Brinna digs her toes in the sand looking for clams with Grandpa, and she cooks the clams with Nana so everyone can have steamers and dip them in little cups of melted butter. One time Grandpa found a white crab the size of a grown man's hand and he stabbed it through with a stick and then held it up, a crab-sicle, with all its legs kicking out from its sides. Nana put the crab in the steamer pot, and Brinna heard it rattling around in there, looking for a way out. The grownups each took a leg and dug and pulled out smooth white cylinders of meat, but Brinna didn't want one. Not even when Daddy dipped a piece and held it glistening in front of her so a drop of yellow fell down onto the table like a tiny midday sun. He shrugged his shoulders and said, "Your loss," and she watched his jaw move as he chewed it up.

There are kids to play with at Nana and Grandpa's house. In the summertime there are more, but even now, between Thanksgiving and Christmas, there are kids at the Rosas' down the street, and maybe at the Palermos' on the beach. Daddy punches the radio until a woman's voice talks about highways on the way to Boston. "It's rough going on 495," she says through a sprinkle of static, "slippery out there," and Brinna squeezes her hands hard together in an effort to be good, as she often does as soon as Thanksgiving is over and it's only a cold month's worth of time until Christmas and presents. She wants skates this year, not figure skates but the kind that will let her go faster than light, the kind that will let her fly. She squeezes and wants to ask Daddy why his eyes are red, but she can't tell if this is a rude question. She doesn't want her skates to hang in the balance.

Last year, in the second grade, Finn Marshall told her there was no such thing as Santa Claus. He'd been almost crying. "I know," Brinna had said, because she'd always known. She'd never believed in the Easter Bunny or the Tooth Fairy either. When her parents speak of Santa, she plays along because she does not know how to say they can stop anytime. If Patrick believes in Santa when he gets old enough to walk and talk and recognize the things in the world that he wants, she'll pretend for him too. For reasons unknown, it makes her parents happy.

She doesn't mind knowing for sure about Santa. What she hates is knowing about God. If there is no Tooth Fairy, only her mother sliding a dollar under her pillow while Brinna pretends to be asleep, and no leprechauns or unicorns, then it makes sense there are no angels, and if no angels, then no devil and definitely no God. But that's not what her parents believe. She doesn't understand how they can say God gave them a child with a broken heart and then love that same God anyway. It makes as much sense as saying "Tooth Fairy" but keeping Brinna's teeth in a jelly jar high up in their medicine cabinet where she can see them through the glass.

So instead of asking about Daddy's red eyes, Brinna takes her cold nose away from the window and asks where the men took Patrick. It's not the first time he's gone in an ambulance, and it's not the first time she's been taken to Grandpa and Nana's while Mama and Daddy go wherever Patrick went, but it's the first time her mother didn't say goodbye first.

"Boston," Daddy says into the rearview. "I'll go there too after you're settled."

"Okay," Brinna says. At Nana's house she will make snow pies and snow angels and snow ladies and snowballs. She will walk to the Rosas', and if Francesca has a snow day too, they will pelt each other with handfuls of the cold white crystals until both are wet and chilled and cherry-cheeked. Then they will sit on Nana's gray tweed couch and watch cartoons with milk and Nana's macarons. Nana will smoke outside, and Grandpa will go to the basement where he keeps the baby tomato shoots until he can plant them in a ring around the house in spring. Brinna tries to count the snowflakes out the window as they pass, but of course there are too many.

The phone at Nana's house rings in the middle of *Duck Tales*. Nana answers it and stretches the long cord so she can talk in the hall. She isn't out there very long before she comes back into the living room and sets the receiver in its cradle.

"Okay, girls," she says, clapping hands wrinkled like wet laundry. "Get bundled."

Brinna's fingers and toes are still chilled from sliding for hours down the hill behind Nana's house and then getting pulled on a wooden sled with red metal runners around roads frozen almost to ice by Francesca's oldest brother, Salvi. If Brinna had her skates already, she would have pulled Salvi and Franny through the streets fast as a jet. When Salvi got tired, he'd dropped them off at Brinna's grandparents'. Franny has four brothers, total: Anthony is after Salvi, then after Franny come Dom and Nicky. Nicky seems to live in his high chair. Whenever Brinna visits, he is always there clapping chubby hands covered in applesauce or oatmeal, grinning with empty gums.

Nana steps in front of the television, blocking out Launchpad McQuack, who ogles the wreckage of a crashed plane in which he's miraculously escaped harm.

"Bundle, girls," Nana says. "Now." She snaps off the TV and shakes the melted snow from Brinna's coat, scooping up Brinna's Barbie backpack full of coloring books and crayons.

Francesca picks up her scarf from a chair near the front door with two fingers. It is snow-soaked and dripping onto the plastic mat. "Yucky yuck," Francesca says.

Draped in wet outer things, they walk with Nana to Franny's through a thick fall of snow. There, the warmth and peace of Nana's living room are replaced by tumbled, boy-noise confusion and a hectic kind of heat. The younger boys are on the family room floor with matchbox cars and an elaborate road system featuring two different loop-de-loops and a giant sloping straightaway. Brinna thinks herself small. She would be able to take those loops, she thinks, as long as she got a good enough head start. She is standing in the doorway, hearing the whisper of her blades on the narrow track, which would be ice from wall to retaining wall and lined with spectators. She'd bend her knees and keep her body close to the ground, leaning forward, like the skaters she saw on TV. She'd pump her arms and feel air burn in through her nose, down her windpipe, filling her chest like a balloon.

Franny's mother has big round cheeks and round shoulders. Draped in a rust-colored dress and many layers of scarves and shawls, she looks like a spool of thread drawn large. Francesca peels off her hat and gloves, her scarf and coat, and they walk to the bathroom, dumping their coats in the dry bathtub.

Franny goes to the room she shares with the littlest boys and returns with two sweatshirts. Brinna gets the one showing puffy cats at play.

"Thanks," Nana says in the other room with Franny's mother. "For taking her like this."

Brinna shrugs the sweatshirt on and goes back in the noisy living room. In the parents' bedroom Mr. Rosa is building something with a hammer and nails, and in the living room a cop show blares on TV, the kind of show Brinna isn't allowed to watch at home. The boys slam their metal cars into each other, crying out each time they collide. And in the kitchen there is something sizzling without Franny's mother there to watch it, something crackling like a giant pot of Rice Krispies in milk, a bowl huge enough for the Big Friendly Giant.

"It's nothing," Mrs. Rosa says. Nicky, the baby, balanced on her hip, is gleefully pulling on her hair. He raises fists full of brown strands toward the ceiling and laughs, face smeared in something green. Spinach, Brinna thinks, or pistachio ice cream. Mrs. Rosa bounces him on her hip, saying, "What's one more?"

Nana kneels before Brinna, a grimace twisting her lips as her knee lands in carpet. "Be a good girl for Mrs. Rosa," Nana says, smoothing back Brinna's hair until her thick curls loosen and expand, puffing in the wake of her grandmother's damp palm.

"For how long?" Brinna asks. She likes Francesca, likes her family, but she wanted to finish *Duck Tales*. Wanted another cookie.

Nana shakes her head. Her face is somehow full, as if it will crack open any minute, and she speaks in short, tight bursts. "Don't know," she says, more wrinkles growing around her mouth and eyes. "Someone will get you before bedtime."

The sky outside is still full of the white snow light, and night seems far away. "Daddy will get me?" she says, and Nana stands, leaning on the sofa arm, then gives Brinna a rough hug. "Don't know," Nana says.

Brinna and Franny help clean up after a dinner of ravioli, little tubes of brown meat filled with grainy cheese, crusty bread with a squishy middle, hot and buttered, and canned corn that Brinna was allowed to push around her plate instead of eat. At the end of dinner Mr. Rosa slid his chair back from the table. "Back to work," he said, the tails of his moustache lifting when he smiled. There were only six chairs around the table, and all the girls got their own, so Salvi had taken little Dom on his lap. Mrs. Rosa fed Nicky in his high chair until tomato specks spotted his cheeks and chin.

After the boys are gone, the air in the kitchen gets lighter and everyone becomes busy. Franny stacks the plates and stands on a stool to fill the sink with water and soap, while Brinna works at scooping leftovers into square plastic boxes that will stack up on top of each other in the fridge. Mrs. Rosa wipes a damp cloth over

Nicky's mouth, then swipes at the table and the counters, getting the worst of the crumbs and the smudges.

"Now," she says. "Doughnuts."

Franny drops the last plate back into the soapy water and cheers. The plate makes a splash that needs paper towels and dish cloths to mop it up. "Doughnuts," Franny says, her face an exclamation point. "We only have those on Christmas."

Brinna sits at the table and watches Mrs. Rosa half fill a black metal pot with oil. She puts it on one of the green stove's back burners and turns it on high. From the refrigerator she pulls a plastic bag containing three packets of dough wrapped in wax paper.

"I made this after breakfast. No real reason," Mrs. Rosa says. She pushes a packet across the clean table to Brinna.

Brinna doesn't know what to do, but she watches Mrs. Rosa and Franny as they unwrap the paper and work the dough with their fingers until it is soft, until the chill almost all gives way. Franny and her mother pull pieces from it. Some they shape like pretzels, some they simply twist, some they hollow out the center so it looks like a real doughnut from a real store. When there is a big tray of their creations, Mrs. Rosa lifts the lid on the pot of shimmering oil and drops several of the dough shapes in. She fixes paper plates of powdered sugar, tiny chocolate chips, and cinnamon sugar in the middle of the table. After a few minutes have passed, she fishes the golden doughnuts from the oil, sets them to drain on paper towels, and starts a new batch frying.

"Dig in," she says. "Girls get first pick." When Mrs. Rosa turns to the side, Brinna can see the way her stomach pushes out beyond the rest of her. It's the way Brinna's mother looked a year ago when she was big with Patrick inside her.

Brinna takes a soft, heart-shaped piece of dough, hot enough still to burn her fingers, and drops it on the cinnamon-sugar plate, then flips it. The girls take their prizes into the living room and all the boys are in there, lying across the flowered sofa or kicking their heels in the air watching a rerun of *Full House.*

"There's doughnuts," Franny says, and the girls take spots on the couch where Salvi has been sprawled. The boys trip over each other on their way to the kitchen, shouting.

Brinna's doughnut is crisp on the outside where her teeth dig in, chewy and sweet and warm in the middle. The sugar dissolves on Brinna's tongue, and she chews happily, stopping occasionally to lick her fingers or to grin at Franny, who has a spattering of white powder like a clown's makeup across her cheeks. Even Baby Nicky gets one, squeezing it in one fist and gumming it to a gooey, stringy mess that coats his hands and chubby arms.

Mr. Rosa stops pounding in the big bedroom and disappears into the kitchen. "What's all this?" he says, a loud voice hovering like thunder over all the other smaller noises. On the television Brinna watches a pair of blond sisters sit on a couch with their legs sticking straight out, just like she and Franny are sitting on the Rosas' flowered couch. Between the blond girls is a baby Nicky's age, Patrick's age, only the one on TV is a girl with pink cheeks.

"What is your father making in there?" Brinna says. Mr. Rosa has emerged from the kitchen with three doughnuts in a napkin, wiping one hand on the belly of his T-shirt, and now there is pounding again in the big room out of sight.

Franny stands up to go for seconds. "A crib for the new baby," she says. "It's another girl, finally."

To get to the kitchen, the girls have to step over a game of Hungry Hungry Hippos that Anthony and Dom have started next to their matchbox track, and Salvi cuts in front of them to scoop up Nicky, prying the slimy doughnut from the baby's tight grip. "That's enough for you," says Salvi, who is ten and tall. He puts the baby to bed.

Brinna and Francesca watch all of *TGIF.* Bedtime comes and goes. After the last show is over, Mrs. Rosa makes Franny get into her jammies and sends her off to sleep. On the couch, Brinna closes her eyes. Before sleep comes, she hears Salvi's music from the room he shares with Anthony. Mr. Rosa bellows for him to shut it off. Franny's sleepy giggle comes through her closed door, and the bedsprings in that room shake from little Dom jumping on their mattress.

Earlier, Franny said her family would move in the spring to a new house with more rooms. There were just too many kids, with one on the way, to stay in this tiny house. Brinna said nothing. All she could think about was having to make new friends when she visited Nana and Grandpa. No more supersoakers on summer days. No more of Mrs. Rosa's lemonade. No more house full of happy family noises.

When Brinna's father shakes her awake, the living room is silent and warm and empty. Mrs. Rosa comes out of the kitchen with a thermos for her father and a couple of doughnuts wrapped up in paper towels. She is crying, which makes Brinna's eyes get wet too.

"Here," Mrs. Rosa says, handing the treats to Brinna. "Carry these, okay?"

They cross the living room rug, which has been cleared of cars and trucks and plastic keys and socks and board games and Barbie clothes. Brinna hugs Mrs. Rosa goodbye. She says, "You make good doughnuts," and Mrs. Rosa smiles but doesn't stop crying.

In the car, Daddy opens the thermos and takes a swig before starting the engine. The coffee smell pricks Brinna's nose. It reminds her of the sunny mornings when Daddy has all day to stay at home and he comes to wake her up, sitting by her bed.

"We're going home, right, Daddy?" Brinna is cold, wrapped up in her outdoor clothes, which are mostly dry now, except for the scarf which is wool and damp and tickly.

"We're going to see your mother," Daddy says. "And Patrick. In the hospital."

There's no music and no crackly news on the radio, so Brinna falls asleep in the backseat with the seatbelt still around her middle, her head against one door and her legs curled up underneath her coat. As she falls into sleep, the cooled doughnuts fall to the backseat floor, where she will find them in the morning coated in sand and salt and mud. When she wakes again, it is still dark, and she is being carried, her head on Daddy's shoulder, her jacket unzipped and loosened, mittens dangling on their metal clips.

This is a different hospital from the one where Brinna's arm got fixed. Nana and Grandpa are in a small waiting room together. He has his arm around her. When Nana sees Brinna and Daddy, she turns her face away, into Grandpa's shoulder. In another small room, Mama is sitting in a rocking chair by a clear plastic crib. Patrick lies inside with his eyes closed. He wears only a diaper. His little chest moves sharply up and down.

"Honey," Mama says. Daddy puts her in Mama's lap, and Mama's arms go around her. Patrick is small and sick and broken. Mama rocks and rocks.

"He's dreaming," Mama says into Brinna's hair. "I can tell by his face it's a good one."

They rock and rock together, and Daddy sits with his hands in one big fist between his knees. There is a machine next to Patrick that makes a slicing noise, like a speed skater moving ahead of the pack. The floors in this room are shiny and slick and good for skating. Brinna wants to take Patrick's crib and push him around, push him through the hallways on her slick, fast feet. She wants to skate in circles down the hallways, out into the snowstorm so he can feel the feather flakes landing on his face. She wants to skate him back to the Rosas' house and sit him on the red rug with Baby Nicky and all the Rosa children, the ones who know how to breathe and eat, whose hearts know how to pump, whose hearts have the right amount of rooms. Brinna wants to take Patrick's hand and put a doughnut in it, and watch it get gummy in his open mouth. Brinna is glad the Rosas are moving. They are too many and too lucky and too nice.

"It's not fair," Brinna says. She pushes herself off Mama's lap and stands with her nose against Patrick's clear crib. It's not fair that Mrs. Rosa gets all the babies she wants. Brinna is still wearing Franny's cat sweatshirt. It smells of the Rosas' house. "This isn't fair."

"Me and God, we're having a tug-of-war," Mama says. She pets Brinna's hair like her daughter is one of cats on the borrowed shirt. Heaven still feels to Brinna like the North Pole, like a place the *Duck Tales* gang might go, Launchpad McQuack flying them there by accident in his crazy airplane. But Brinna wishes she could believe, for her mother. She wishes she could believe that if Patrick doesn't open his eyes and gurgle in the way that means he's hungry, then he might open his eyes in another world instead, one with a gentle old man and all the cold teething rings Patrick could ever want. But Brinna knows what happens when she falls asleep. There is only darkness. She never remembers her dreams.

Brinna puts a small hand on her mother's face. The skin there is cool and spongy. There is no room for God in this white, humming room. There is no room for Him in Brinna's heart. She thinks the word "hate" and feels it slice through her like an actual knife. It makes her shiver, and her mother tightens her arms around Brinna's middle. Her mother's arms are strong, so it's a good thing Brinna is sturdy. Sometimes a nurse with a ponytail or a doctor with a turned-down smile comes in to talk to Mama, but mostly they wait: Mama in the rocking chair and Brinna napping in her lap; Daddy on the empty made-up bed; Nana and Grandpa leaning against each other, propped up by the doorway. The dark outside the window gets lighter and bluer and clearer and colder as they wait to see if Patrick will wake.

Make Way for Her

Early inhabitants dubbed the springs "strange and mysterious waters"—a seemingly accurate name because in some
locations spring water appears somewhat magically from the
ground, runs downstream for several yards, and then disappears mysteriously below the surface once again.

—"Florida's Cool Springs and Wild Rivers," sierraclub.org

Last week my teenager's best friend died after taking a pill she
thought was Molly, a pure form of the active ingredient in Ecstasy.
It was a pink pill stamped with a tiny imprint of a heart, my teenager told me in the ER, where I had been summoned at 2:15 in the
morning.

My teenager had also taken one of the pills, she told me in
the waiting room, all her limbs folded at their creases in a way
that turned her body to envelope, a smooth and private recepta-
cle neatly concealing an unknown number of luminous sins. She
had thrown it up, though, thank God, along with the Niçoise salad
we'd shared before she left for the concert. Too many vodka Red
Bulls, she told me without shame, wheedled out of too many hopeful of-age men.

"We should still get you checked out," I told her, the scuffed
leather purse on my lap weighting me to the seat in the room where

we waited for Kendra's parents. They lived all the way across town in a graceful neighborhood shielded on all sides by live oaks and Spanish moss.

My teenager switched the set of her crossed arms over her birdbone chest. She wore her father's old army jacket, a covering fetched from the car when I saw the way she shivered in her sequined top beneath a framed print of *Starry Night*. The last time we shared this waiting room, two years ago, I'd been cradling her on my lap. She'd gotten down to eighty-two pounds and had passed out, hitting her head on the coffee table. We were past all that now, though.

"It came up whole," she said. "I remember thinking, there goes fifty bucks, literally down the toilet."

Another mother might have forced her to the admitting nurse, secured a curtained gurney, begged for a tox screen, a stomach pump, but I believed her. She had not lied about the concert, after all. I'd let her go, even though it was seventeen and up. I wasn't even angry about the drinks. At least she'd told me. Secrets were a bad sign. Secrets led to skipping dinner because she "already ate." They led to three exorbitant weeks at Canopy Cove with equine therapy and twenty-four-hour supervision.

And my teenager did not shake or twitch or sweat now, as her friend had done before the ambulance was called. My teenager picked at her purple-painted nails and did not cry, because the death was occurring out of sight, in another realm of reality that would have no bearing on her life until the Wednesday wake, the stares in the halls, the cell phone mute on her hip.

Last night my teenager sat on a stool at the kitchen bar, her laptop a flimsy shield between us while I sliced peppers for stir-fry. "Is your paper done?" I asked. Something on the fall of the Roman Empire. I had to watch her for the answer, which came in the form of a shrug.

"Pepper?" I held out one long green question mark, and she

pinched it between her fingers without looking away from her screen. Slowly she brought the tip of it between her teeth and bit, chewed slowly, then set the rest on the counter. I tried not to calculate the vitamin content in two centimeters of bell pepper.

"Your father's going to be late again. Set the table for you and me, okay?"

My teenager finally looked at me with all the sentience of a blank piece of paper. She closed her computer without saving whatever she'd been writing and laid her head on top of its humming smoothness. Hair dyed the red of maple leaves fanned itself over her face.

Six days she'd been this way, closemouthed to words and food, yet always keeping me in sight. While I deadheaded roses, she slumped in the porch swing. As I separated recyclables, she lingered in the garage with me, lifting and resetting her father's hammers on their wall pegs. Every time I came out of the shower, she was lying in a heap on my bed.

My husband is an engineer. He has tried to fix the problem with ice cream. With the church of his childhood that I do not attend. With serious discussions about the varied side effects of recreational drugs. With a new iPad. With the purchase of a scrapbooking kit that sits on her bedroom floor, still shrink-wrapped, slowly accumulating a coating of worn socks gray on their bottoms. His new plan seems to involve once again retreating to the cubicle where he spent most of his time before the accident, leaving me and our teenager essentially alone.

Today is the first Saturday of October in Tallahassee, a place where summer resists the fall with a child's grudge against bedtime. A full week after.

When I wake, my teenager is not on the sofa where she'd fallen asleep. Her car, which has not been driven since the Spangler concert, sits in the driveway under a layer of needles from the paternal pine tree hunching above. Inside again, I tear back shower curtains and peer in the laundry room, checking all the places where heat and lightheadedness have in the past conspired to bring her down. Finally, back in my bedroom, I shake my husband awake. "Raymond," I say, but even as he begins to surface and blink, I see one pink sole curled against the carpet and bend to find her sprawled flat beneath our bed, face flushed in sleep.

"S'kay, Jeannie," Ray says. He blows out his lips in sleep, horselike. "Jus' a bad dream."

I go down on protesting knees so I can reach one hand to her forehead before squeezing her ankle with the other. When she tries to sit up, the bones in my fingers crunch between the crown of her head and the edge of the bed frame, and still she says nothing, conveying all her shock of waking into the same old terrifying universe with her walnut-wide brown eyes.

"Come with me," I tell her. "We're going out."

She lies back down, but after I begin to bustle around, yanking jeans from a drawer, shrugging into a sweatshirt, she steals into the hall and I hear the bathroom door click closed.

At Starbucks, I get her favorite green tea smoothie, but she just stares out her window, palms up in her lap like a Buddhist monk in prayer. Most of the leaves over the tunneled canopy roads are still green. When we pass the farmers' market in the chain of parks running like an emerald vein across Tallahassee's belly, the car fills with the burned sugar smell of kettle corn.

In her pigtailed single digits, my teenager's favorite place on earth was a mile-long spring in Wakulla County where alligators sunned on muddy banks a hundred yards from the roped-off swimming area, and where all manner of egrets and spoonbills and moorhens and warblers nested and fed and fought in the underbrush, and where, in the spring, manatees mugged for the tour boats in water clear enough to make out every dip and ridge of the weed-dotted silty bottom.

"It's too cold to swim," she says, when I take the last turn before the springs.

"The boats run all day," I say, careful not to whoop or grin at her first words since the night Kendra collapsed at The Moon and the band just kept on playing. "We'll take a tour."

It's a weekend, so the pavilions overflow with birthday parties on the wide lawn between the lodge and the spring. Grills sizzle with sausages and caramelizing onions, smelling of a county fair. Kids run and turn handsprings, chasing each other beneath the faded sign touting one of the park's archaic attractions, Henry the Pole-Vaulting Fish, done in kitschy fifties style. Balloons anchored to picnic tables jostle in the breeze like bubbles in a glass of champagne.

There are twenty minutes until the next tour begins, so we park ourselves on a bench in the loading dock with a dozen other passengers, watching kids wade on the other side of the fence where the water's green silk nibbles at a white-sand shore. One little boy, about four, has his jeans rolled to mid-thigh and shivers visibly, lips edged in dusky blue as he cups what he can of the spring and flings it at an older girl, his sister maybe. As we watch, she digs a piece of driftwood from the muck and uses it to scoop up double the water his little hands can hold.

"When was the last time we were here?" I ask my teenager, hoping for more words.

She too watches the children play. Their parents are not obvious on the small beach. So much time passes that I touch her shoulder. Even after all her progress, it's nothing more than a knob of bone beneath a crepe-paper-thin T-shirt. "Was it your birthday?"

She shrugs that compact shoulder, then brings up the cuff of the Leon High sweatshirt looped around her waist to jab at one of her eyes. It comes away with two perfect circles of wet.

"It was warm," I say, talking myself into the memory. "I got a milkshake in the lodge."

The kids have stopped splashing now. The little girl has run out of the water. She has been holding up her dress and now, when she lets it fall, she's almost dry, good as new, but the little boy wraps himself in an imperfect hug, blue jeans heavy and dark with wet, feet powdered above the ankle with white sand. I'm standing before I realize it, unzipping my sweatshirt to toss it over the fence, when a woman in short white shorts crosses the beach. "Soup's on. Come and get a plate, Darryl," she says, and he waddles faster, chasing her back to the biggest pavilion.

"Mom," my teenager calls from behind me. I force my fingers to release the fence's black bars. "Boat's loading."

"Lucky if he doesn't catch pneumonia," I say as we follow the others down the metal ramp, which sings with the rhythm of our steps. The sky overhead is perfectly white, unmarked.

"So now you're a doctor?" My teenager walks before me, hair cordoning off the sides of her face like blinders. She was up to one hundred pounds at her physical last month, happier than I'd ever seen her, buoyed by a new love of music and singing in the choir where Ray takes her to Mass.

"Of course not," I say. Heat rushes to my jaw. In the hospital's waiting room, my teenager asked if Kendra suffered, or if it was like going to sleep. She asked if I believed in heaven. I told her I was just a secretary—going on twenty years in the dean's office—not a doctor. I said there were things it might be better never to know. Now I say, "I don't have to be a doctor to know it's too cold to be messing around in the water. You said it yourself."

She relapses into silence and steps from dock to flat-bottomed boat, finally sitting on the right side, halfway back behind the driver so she can look into the dense growth at the water's edge where snakes and gators and cooters and occasional deer haunt the banks. I slide in next to her, studying her perfect ear studded with three silver balls, the metallic red of her flyaway hair.

Tomorrow she'll sing of Christ risen at Good Shepherd, but today she'll sail with me through a green cathedral where the fallen log gives rise to the mushroom that will feed the squirrel destined for the belly of a water moccasin. It's the only kind of heaven I know.

"It was too thick to drink," I say, remembering the Oreo milkshake from our last visit, the chunks that clogged my oversized red straw. "I had to suck so hard I got dizzy, remember? Then you tried, and your face almost turned inside out."

My teenager is shaking her head as the boat backs out and the driver/guide begins his spiel: "Welcome to Wakulla Springs, home of Tarzan and the Creature from the Black Lagoon, preserver of mastodon bones and whatever lies one hundred ninety feet down on the floor of its ancient basin—"

"I went and got you a spoon," she says, fighting the way her lips want to curve and part and spread into a smile.

"Take note, ladies and gents," the guide drones, "of the osprey nest up ahead."

She knows my father died when I was young enough for my memories of him to end at the shoulders, though by all accounts he was not a tall man. I've brought my teenager here to remind her that even in death we are in life, and that the best way to honor the dead is to live full lives ourselves. In our memories, we bear them with us. When my father died, that was the path my mother chose. It's always made more sense to me than an ongoing toga party in the sky.

"Sweetie," I say, and tuck a hank of her red hair—chestnut brown underneath all that dye—behind her studded ear. "I know how hard this week has been." Her eyes are liquid brown, a color she longs to change with contacts, violet, in two years when she turns eighteen.

Her lashes grow wet as I watch. Her mouth opens, but just then the guide throws the engine in reverse and brings the boat to a standstill. I'm nodding at my teenager. Go on, please go on, but she's turning, looking out her side of the boat where the other passengers have clustered to stare openmouthed at a gator, "a relatively small bull animal, only about twelve feet," the guide says, pointing out the splintered shaft of an arrow emerging from its hide, the remains of a failed assassination. The gator too is openmouthed.

"Take a good look folks," the guide intones. "These guys are secretive about hunting. Twelve years I've sailed this river, and I've never seen one take prey."

We watch the gator, camouflaged by the bank's leafy expanse of fern and bald-top cypress knees, as the gator watches us, great snout agape, dull white teeth stalactites opposite stalagmites in a pink cave that hides within it, it seems, a second mouth: delicate, vulnerable, a pale silk purse to keep safe all struggling deposits. And its prey, an orange-beaked moorhen ducking its head beneath the surface among a stand of reeds, oblivious to danger in its hunger.

"We'll give it another minute," the guide says, voice taut with the triumph of presenting us this tableau. "These guys'll spend hours, sometimes, just like this, waiting—"

To spring. To attack. To strike. To feed. Whatever the guide says next is drowned by the single thrust of the creature's massive tail, the resulting wave, the smack of its spring-loaded jaw. The sound my teenager makes is half gasp, half sob, backing into me so my arms can cross ineffectually over her, at last holding her breakable body against my chest. Her breath hitches there, back rising and falling against me, stuttering like the boat's engine roaring to life beneath us. I'm holding her tight, rocking us side to side, peering over her shoulder when I see it, the moorhen jigging out of the reeds, head bobbing, candy-corn beak parted to issue a shrill warning.

"It got away," I say, pointing to the creature. "Look, sweetie, it's fine."

The gator hovers now, nostrils and eyes showing through the thin scrim of water, scaly back like a mat of braided weeds stretching out behind. "Looks like it's a lucky day for everybody but the gator, folks," the guide says into his microphone.

My teenager's breath has slowed now, and she moves politely out of my grip. The boat slinks along the bank as mullet flash out of the water alongside us in little silver commas.

I can feel the grief still inside her. An anchor buried in mud. "That was something," I say.

"It was my birthday," she says, and I can almost smell the spring drying on her skin the last time we were here. She'd been jumping from the diving tower in a bikini that stood out yellow against a blue screen of sky. We went to the lodge after she dried off. She and Kendra, who'd worn a red one-piece, black braids coiled in an elegant heap on her head.

"You had a brownie sundae," I say.

"And she had a banana split," my teenager finishes for me, one hand, so small, all bones, rising to grip the rail.

"I'm so, so sorry, sweetie," I say. "Please, tell me what I can do to help."

She shakes her head, mouth pressed to a thin pink line. "God, Mom," she says, hands now tiny fists in her lap. "We took it once before, and it was fine. This time it wasn't. End of story."

The boat enters the final green corridor, returning to the dock. Life teems on either side, ruffling the leaves of the cypress trees, burrowing into loam, ribboning underneath us.

As is her habit at this point in the tour, she leans over the edge of the boat while we glide toward the deepest part of the spring. If this were a sunny day and the water clear enough, we'd be able to see the caves ringing the bottom where ten million gallons of water flood into the basin each hour, every drop carrying along infinitesimal grains of Florida's limestone foundation, slowly undermining the solid-seeming ground where we build our homes, where we let our children run barefoot across green lawns. Today the water's surface is a blank silver.

"You and Dad should try it sometime," she says. In the thickening mist, the diving tower is abandoned. "You don't think. You just are. You love everyone. And everyone is beautiful."

The guide pilots the boat expertly back to the dock where we will disembark, and my teenager burrows into her sweatshirt. We emerge into a light rain, and her uncovered hair fills with diamond flecks. We walk past the deserted beach, toward the emptying pavilions. I try to imagine my Raymond on Ecstasy. He might like it, actually, if he didn't have a chance to brace himself against it. When we met, he'd liked his weed. I'd be too focused on the science behind the drug to let it in, though. I'd try to chart the dopamine flood, map the damage to my gray matter, analyze all that could go wrong.

"When my father died," I tell her, "everyone said it happened for a reason. Part of His unknowable plan. My mother didn't accept that. We had to find our own way through. I guess you do, too."

At the largest pavilion, most of the balloons have burst and hang down from their strings like strange, withered fruit. A few adults bend over picnic tables, collecting plates littered with cake crumbs. The woman in the white shorts sits at one table, facing out, the little boy from the beach bundled in a plaid blanket and balanced on her lap, fast asleep there. She rocks him absently, stealing glances at his thin, slack-jawed face. The currents that feed the spring run under their feet and mine. Under those of my daughter in her checkered slip-on shoes.

"You should know, I'm going to do stupid stuff sometimes," she says, my teenager, hands deep in her sweatshirt pockets. "But I promise to try not to make the same mistake twice."

Every so often in this water-rimmed state, the ground crumbles beneath our feet, draining lakes and swallowing houses, plucking sleepers from their beds even as they dream.

"I'm starving," I say. The urge to fill myself, to weigh myself down, is sudden and strong.

Her face is turned down to her cell phone, which lights at the touch of her thumb. She laughs at something she reads there, then shakes the hair out of her face to look at me.

"We could stop for lunch, if you want," she says. "I kind of feel like pizza."

I pretend to consider while she digs white earbuds out of her pocket and plugs them in one at a time, beginning to nod to some music I can hear only as a distant whine. In a moment it has taken her over. She spins in its embrace, eyes closed as she mouths something along with the singer, twirling in the rain, expecting the world to make way for her as it always has, trusting that it always will, lucky that this time it does.

Silent Blooms of Sudden Heat

Finally, it was summer. Soon Brie would spend afternoons behind the counter at her father's bike rental business, signing out beach cruisers to tourists whose expensive cologne stuck to the twenties they peeled from their billfolds. For now, though, the tedium of algebra was past, and so too the excruciating periods of language lab, where she was always the last to find a conversation partner with whom to discuss in halting present-tense Spanish the rising humidity and traffic influx signaling Cape Cod's transition into June.

As a child, Brie had anticipated summer with the certainty that each week would bring new wonders—a trip to Buttonwood Park Zoo, a double feature at the Wellfleet Drive-In where she could never keep from falling asleep during the second movie, a crack-of-dawn fishing trip reeling up fluke with her dad and the boy cousins, all of whom were older and called her Starfish and Buttercup instead of the insults kids had been flinging at her on the playground since Gregory Watson had discovered her name was a kind of French cheese. No matter that the etymology worked out to "the exalted one" in Gaelic and English, Gregory and his crew dubbed her Cheese Pie or Limburger or sometimes simply the Funk. For most of her life, summers meant escaping their notice.

Now, though, as sophomores, those boys had transitioned to torturing her more developed contemporaries. Babs McDonnell became Boobs Magee, and Brenda Buchard was Buttalicious, while Lindsey *Freaking* Laine acquired a new middle name among boys bragging about their encounters with the most beautiful girl in tenth grade. With waist-length platinum hair and more curves than a corkscrew, she would have been striking even if she didn't have the singing voice rippling with vibrato that had earned her the lead in both musicals during her tenure, so far, at Hyannis High.

When Brie signed on as assistant stage manager for *Once Upon a Mattress,* she'd thought it an easy means of satisfying three arts credits. She figured Lindsey would be involved, but was as surprised as anyone when a friendship sprang up between them. Between backstage quick changes and late-night rehearsals, running lines during free and the final cast party, Brie was drawn inexorably into Lindsey's inner circle. They had a remarkable number of things in common, like a secret passion for *Star Trek* reruns and a taste for Sour Patch Kids. They'd both memorized all the jokes from *Airplane!,* an old movie they'd watched one night after they'd torn through their Netflix DVDs—the mere mention of the word "surely" could send them into a full Leslie Nielsen impression. They often walked home from school together, stopping at the mall to try on impossibly steep stilettos and squirt each other with four kinds of perfume and parade through the food court speaking in cartoonish British accents for no reason.

For the first time, Brie became visible to HHS's Cool Elite, among them boys who ceased hurling their cheese-based insults and now called her Easy-Breezy as they passed in the halls. She was 90 percent sure the new nickname signaled affection.

Brie's phone flashed Lindsey's name five days before school let out. Despite the respite from classes, Brie was nervous about the summer break. While Brie was making change for tourists in the dim of her father's shop, Lindsey would be bouncing from camps for drama, basketball, and leadership to a ten-day tour of Europe with her parents that she claimed to want to skip.

How could their fledgling friendship hold up under those conditions? Wasn't it likely Brie would endure three sticky months of swabbing vinyl bike seats, minding her brothers and sister, suffering the sneers of visiting rich kids, and waiting for Lindsey to infuse the life back into life, only to find that her new friend had moved on to new friends? Brie was apparently forgettable, judging by the way the 4-H girls Brie still saw at weekly meetings had stopped inviting her to their movie marathons and thrifting, sensing a Lindsey-fueled defection.

Lindsey called after dinner from her family's beachfront castle. That structure was a wonder Brie had toured sparingly, since Lindsey preferred to crash in Brie's musty basement. While littered with her brothers' matchbox cars, it boasted an unalarmed bulkhead, which enabled the girls to sneak out to parties where Brie had learned to sip one beer all night and pretend to get as drunk as everyone else.

"Come to Florida with me," Lindsey said as soon as Brie answered. "Say you can. It's the last fun I'll have before all the crap my parents are forcing on me this summer."

"Florida?" Brie asked. She had never ventured beyond the confines of New England. There had never been a need. All her extended family lived within a two-hour drive, and she'd already been born in a place where others saw fit to vacation at the edge of an ocean Brie considered the beginning and end of what was beautiful. Lindsey's family had time-shares in Hawaii and Aspen in addition to Florida. Since she was an only child, Lindsey explained, she had a standing arrangement that she could bring two friends to distract her while her parents drank and dined and went on overnight jaunts and generally acted as if they didn't have a kid and didn't intend to. Lindsey's malleable voice sounded simultaneously disappointed and forgiving, and somehow not at all bitter.

"You're sure you want me to come?" Brie asked, grasping her cell with two hands as if the question lent it a terrible weight.

Lindsey's answer splintered into a thousand glittery pieces. "Of course!" she said. "Who else will harmonize *Rent* with me? Not Maura, thank God; she's tone deaf."

"Maura?" Brie asked. Maura Crawford was another of Lindsey's confidantes. Whenever circumstances demanded that they speak, Maura always gazed at a point above Brie's head.

"She likes you a ton," Lindsey said. "You just need money for shopping and clubs."

"Clubs?" Brie was starting to feel like a startled parrot, but was rewarded with another peal of laughter.

"We're going to have a blast. Just say yes."

"I have to ask my parents," she said, unable to repress her hesitation. Until recently she'd had two close friends, 4-H girls who raced to raid the henhouse at the start of each meeting and admitted to being "weird," a designation amounting to a particular brand of isolating and self-sustaining dorkiness that privileged Monster-fueled sleepovers over keggers, epic bike rides down the Cape Cod Rail Trail over dances, and academic achievement above social rank.

Brie loved hanging with Lindsey one-on-one, but something shifted when they ran into her other friends, or the boys who begged Linds to chill on Main Street or down at Sea Street Beach. Lindsey was remarkable, and Brie was average, and she was mostly okay with that. But she was no Maura either, and though she'd never tried being a Fort Lauderdale party girl, she doubted she had it in her.

"Maura's parents already said yes," Lindsey said, breathless with exasperation. "We really want you to come."

For a split second Brie let herself entertain the terrible fantasy that the invitation was part of a plot to complete the humiliation of her childhood, but she forced the thought from her mind. That was just a species of the self-consciousness Lindsey said kept

Brie smothered by her own shadow. "You're hilarious, and those curls—gorgeous," Lindsey told her once a week at least. "It could be you on the stage instead of behind it." On good days, Brie almost believed her.

"I'll ask," Brie said, knowing her parents would agree. They loved Lindsey. Brie knew no one who didn't. When she came back to say she'd received permission, Lindsey's "Yes!" was so loud Brie thought it was in response to something else, a homerun in the same Sox game her father had been watching, a winning scratch-off. But then Lindsey started babbling. "We're going to get you a new wardrobe, hook you up with some hotties. You'll come back strutting."

"Wait—" Brie tried to tell Lindsey that she didn't have a knack for transformation. Or the desire. In order for there to be a stage, some people had to stay behind it.

"Girl, I'm going to crack your shell like an oyster," Lindsey said, hanging up.

Brie flopped back on her bed, gazing into the plastic constellations on her ceiling. Downstairs, her brothers accused each other of cheating at Mario Kart. An announcer droned over the crowd-roar of her dad's game. Brie wouldn't mind if it was just Lindsey, but Maura was the girl who poured everyone shots yet never took her own. She delighted in dreaming up truth-or-dare challenges but never got put on the spot. Most annoying, a mysterious off-Cape boyfriend kept her out of the ever-shifting game of relationship hopscotch, while for months now, Lindsey had been after Brie to date around, as if she'd been declining offers left and right.

Brie wasn't the only sixteen-year-old, she guessed, to never have had a boyfriend, but she might have been the only one to think about boys as little as she did. There had been a few crushes in junior high, silent blooms of sudden heat to be weathered. Now she watched her 4-H friends moon over boys who either did or did not like them back, and she followed the celebrity couples of her grade with marginal interest, but no one gave her the heady, heart-pounding, rainbow vision she'd heard others deep "in like" confess. She was so uninterested in romance that she'd even blurted out to one of the 4-H girls last year, a petite brunette named Katrina with hairless arms, that she might be gay.

"Interesting," Katrina had said. Her mother was a psychologist. "And how does that make you feel?" They were sitting on folding chairs at a regional 4-H Halloween Ball. There had been bobbing for apples. There had been cake. Katrina straightened her witch's hat.

"I don't know," Brie said, watching the crowd—the girls were mostly done up as chaste kittens and fairies, except for one in a brown sack who could have been a potato. "Confused. I might not be."

"There's plenty of precedent for homosexuality in nature. Gay penguins and manatees and sheep. It's literally natural."

Brie's face had gone red. No one was dancing, but the dozen girls ringing the community center's basement ferociously eyed the handful of boys—a Jedi, a ghost, a kid in a polo with a sticker that read *Hello, My Name Is* "Cereal Killer." Meanwhile the boys guzzled candy corn, chortled over inside jokes, and ignored the gaggle of girls while bubble-gum pop hollered from a boom box. If this is romance, Brie thought, what's the point?

"I know it's natural," Brie said. "I just don't know if I am."

Katrina fanned herself with her hat. The heat in the basement was up too high. "Are you, like, attracted to girls?"

Brie examined the flecked tiles where fluorescent light pooled like milk. "I notice whose hair looks nice, and whose jeans are too tight." Whenever Brie found herself observing girls in Bio or at lunch, it always led to an immediate scrutiny of her own body. Were her calves rounder than Callie Marshall's? Did the flesh of Brie's back overflow her jeans like Rhodie Delahunt's?

"Well, it doesn't have to be either/or. Didn't you see *Kinsey*?" Katrina said, checking a text. "My mom's here. See you next week."

Brie watched her cross the dance floor, still unnerved. Later she'd only dared to glance at the summary on IMDb before x-ing out the site on the family computer, then clearing its history. The blurb left her even more bewildered. What would a study of "Sexual Behavior in the Human Male" have to do with her?

In all of high school, Brie had noticed only one guy. Shel Frank played the prince opposite Lindsey. He was okay-looking—brown moppish hair, brown eyes, a layer of brown stubble across his narrow jaw—but something had happened when Brie saw him with a couple of cast members in the parking lot a month back. He'd stripped off a sweatshirt, and the T-shirt underneath didn't quite touch the top of his belted jeans, which clung low on his hips. He'd said something that made the group burst into laughter, and Brie saw a thin line of hair running from the base of his belly button into his jeans. Without warning, a jolt of some sweet pressure had seized inside her like a fist. It stopped her in her tracks before she began to wonder if the laughter was aimed at her and spun on her heel, still clutching the water bottles she'd meant to recycle.

The next time she saw Shel, he'd been about to go onstage for a dance number in the second act. Brie had stared until he turned in the narrow wing. She made a noise, a rat's squeak.

"What, did I forget something?" he asked, patting his pockets.

"I didn't know if you needed this," Brie stuttered, lamely holding out his script, which he'd rolled into a telescope and tucked into the taut ropes of the fly system.

"No, thanks. It's all in here," he said, and tapped his temple before springing onto the stage right on cue. She'd watched the whole number hoping for that feeling to visit her again, but the only thing out of the ordinary was her mouth, dry from the shock of being caught staring.

The guards at Logan had to tell Brie to remove her shoes twice, and she walked through the metal detector before the TSA agent was ready. Lindsey threw her arm around Brie's shoulders at the gate, laughing over the education she was already getting, but Maura mocked each infraction.

"I can't believe you packed a bottle of water in your carry-on. Do you live under a rock?" Maura said with a smile that only made her derision more paralyzing.

Brie busied herself with untangling her headphones. "My family drives everywhere," she said. "It's cheaper than paying for six tickets."

Maura inserted earbuds into her thrice-pierced ears. "Jeez, four kids?" she asked, incredulous. "What are you, Catholic?"

Brie sat up in her vinyl seat as if goosed. She waited to see if Lindsey would tell Maura to back off, but Lindsey had already plugged her own ears, Ke$ha's autotuned wail leaking out. "Actually, yes," Brie said, burrowing into her seat. "I have two brothers and a baby sister. Pheebs is hilarious. She just started walking, but she used to love to hang onto this kitchen stool and bend her knees a bunch, sticking her butt out. It looked like she was pole dancing."

Maura blinked, using one thumb to turn up the volume on her iPhone. Brie's face filled with color. At home, her mother would be herding the kidlets to swimming lessons, Phoebe toddling across the hot sand, squealing in the same pitch as the gulls she chased. Lindsey's parents were at the terminal's bar; as she watched, Lindsey's father slipped a hand beneath her mother's silk shirt and snapped her bra loud enough for Brie to hear the echo.

"They're whores on vacation," Lindsey said from her recumbent slouch. Eyes still closed.

Lindsey's parents stuck around for a day before announcing their intention to head to the Keys. They left a credit card. "Don't try any of that fake ID business, Linds," her mother said. "There's plenty in the liquor cabinet. I don't want to have to bail any of you out of jail." She wheeled a suitcase to the door.

"No boys," her father cautioned. "*Capisce?*" Then he opened his arm and Lindsey went on tiptoe to kiss his yellow-stubbled cheek.

"Sir, yes sir," Lindsey said, closing the condo's door. Then she rubbed her hands together. "Mudslides?"

Maura walked past Brie in a coconut-sunscreen cloud, bare feet suctioning to the tiles as she took glasses from the cupboard. Outside it was eighty-eight, and the only clouds were placed there by skywriters. The remnants of "Cocoa Cabana" still hung in the air.

"That's where Damian works, right?" Maura asked, pointing to the thin wisps.

Lindsey was opening a half gallon of milk. "I don't know if he's still there. It's not like we talk."

"Who's Damian?" Brie asked.

"No one. Just this bouncer," Lindsey said, measuring Kahlúa and vodka in a shot glass featuring a pink flamingo wrapped in a towel reading "Fort Lauderdale is for lovers." She stirred the shot into a glass of milk and sipped from it, then handed it to Brie.

It was 11:30 a.m., and Brie would have preferred orange juice to a cocktail, but she took the drink. It tasted like a milkshake. "He doesn't sound like no one." She looked at Maura over the rim of her glass. Maybe the teasing would earn her some points.

"That's because he's Lindsey's Latin lover," Maura said, stirring her drink with a finger. "*Arriba, arriba.*"

"Don't be provincial," Lindsey said, and the smile withered on Maura's face. Brie felt the seesaw between them tip as Lindsey looked to her again. "D's a nice guy. We hung out a little last summer, that's all. Our main focus this trip is finding someone for you, Brie."

Brie licked coffee-flavored milk off her lips. "Thanks, but I'm saving myself for Shel Frank," she said, and giggled. Without him around it was suddenly possible to remember the toast-colored expanse of his stomach, to imagine the warmth of his skin.

Lindsey went to the balcony, and the other girls followed, plopping down in lounge chairs, feet up on the metal railing. The ocean rolled seven floors below, and the horizon was a blue line it hurt to look at. Brie imagined going down to the beach, strolling along the water's edge, and seeing Shel on a blanket with his family. What a coincidence! A time-share in the same building! She imagined them swimming, the hard board of his stomach against her back, and it happened again, that fist seizing inside her, except this time it lingered sweetly.

"She doesn't know?" Maura asked, bouncing back. She nodded slightly, pleased, like she'd won a round of solitaire.

Lindsey flicked her hair over her shoulder sharply. "Shel's a player, Brie," she said.

Brie's glass was empty except for a ring of creamy liquid that dispersed against the side of the glass when she tipped it. "I know he'd never date me," she said.

If Lindsey said, "Don't sell yourself short," then maybe it was possible after all, but one look at Lindsey, staring into her drink, which was mostly full, told her something was wrong.

"He's a dick, Lin," Maura was saying. "Don't waste another second thinking about him."

"Wait," Brie said, feeling thick, fumbling through dark water. "Did you and Shel—"

Lindsey stood, the glass falling, its contents splashing whitely out. Maura stood too. "Nice one, dipshit," Maura said. "Why don't you stab her in the heart too?"

"I didn't know," Brie said, splayed hands shaking as she bent to collect the shards.

When Brie finally summoned the nerve to open Lindsey's door, she was cross-legged on her bed, face puffy but dry. "It's my fault," Lindsey said, pulling Brie into a tight hug. "It just hurts to talk about it. We dated during last year's musical."

"Oh, God," Brie said. "And you had to play against him this year too."

Maura smirked. It was old news to her.

Lindsey shook her head. "Don't feel bad. He seems nice, but after he gets what he wants, it's on to the next," Lindsey said, plucking at the eyelet comforter. She held Brie's glance with a little smile. "He's damn fine, though. You have good taste."

Maura snorted. "Can we go downstairs? I'm getting paler by the minute."

They spent the afternoon on the beach, swimming and sunning, ate dinner at the Blue Parrot, and then went back upstairs to mix a batch of strawberry daiquiris. "Let Operation Summer Love commence," Lindsey said over the blender's whir.

Maura seemed about to object, but recovered, leaning on the granite-topped bar. "What's your type, Brie? Disheveled puppy dog? A surfer? Plenty of those here."

"I just want to dance," Brie said, panic juggling fistfuls of the fries she'd consumed.

"Let's not put all the pressure on Brie," Lindsey said, pouring the icy mixture into three glasses and licking her fingers. "We each bring someone back or none of us do."

"Adam would kill me," Maura said, plunging a bendy straw into her drink.

"Adam shmadam," Lindsey said, sucking at her straw so her cheekbones went concave. "He's thirty and has a bald spot," she told Brie.

"Thirty?" Brie saw Maura's sunburned face go a shade of tomato. "That's, like, illegal."

"*No way.* Illegal? Why didn't anyone *tell* me?" Maura said. "You are such a dipshit."

But Lindsey was shaking with laughter. "He works at Cumbie's. She met him trying to buy cigarettes."

Brie was laughing now too. Maura's mysterious boyfriend from Wareham was a creepy man-child who, Lindsey went on to say, referred to sex as a "flirt and squirt." Plus, he lived with his grandmother.

"Let's find you someone your own generation," Brie said.

Maura crossed her arms tight over her tank top, studying her pink, painful-looking skin. Brie felt bad for knocking her while she was down, but there was power in in it too, the seesaw tipping back, a feeling not exactly like the pleasant pinch and uprush below her belly button that her daydream had evoked, but similar, and she liked it.

When it was sufficiently late, the horizon a uniform black, Brie shimmied into a green tube dress of Lindsey's and Maura's clear heels. "I don't know," Brie said, turning sideways in the mirror. "I look like something that washed up on the beach."

Lindsey picked up a silk clutch. "You are so funny," she said, leading the way to the elevator and into the night, which had acquired a breeze that made them clutch their bare arms. The Cabana was two blocks away. Lindsey headed to the front of the line.

"Damian's working," she whispered. The trio met him at the red velvet rope. Damian was tall and dark, with an accent that rolled his words forward, tumbling them over each other like the tiny shells in the waves Brie had let buffet her that afternoon.

"I don't believe it. Tell me I'm not dreaming," he said. "Little Miss Lindsey all dolled up." He bent forward to wrap his massive arms around her, black T-shirt straining around his biceps.

"We don't have IDs on us," she said, biting her lower lip. Brie watched, fascinated. She'd never seen Lindsey work her magic at close range.

His mouth hitched to the side. "You can make that up to me later," he said. Then he was reaching down to unhook the rope so they could shimmy inside. Someone stamped their hands with blacklight ink, and then Brie and Maura entered the fray, waiting while Lindsey lingered with Damian. "She's just like her mother sometimes," Maura said.

Brie said nothing, watching spotlights play over the undulating dancers. The comparison to the only dance she'd ever been to—that long-ago 4-H Halloween Ball—was so ludicrous she laughed out loud. As she watched, a tall man on the edge of the dancers picked up a girl with spiky black hair and held her to his pelvis while her legs wound around his waist, clinging there. If Brie didn't know better, she would have thought they were having sex, right there in front of everyone, the way he had his hand against her ass and was stumbling to a pillar, pinning her there, thrusting.

"What are you, some kind of sicko? Don't watch," Maura said just as Lindsey came in, applying lip gloss with a finger.

"D's coming up after his shift," she shouted over the beat, something techno.

"Avoid the copulators," Maura said, linking her arms around both Lindsey and Brie, and making it so they could all laugh. It was the first time, Brie thought, that they had all felt the same way about one thing. Following Lindsey to the bar, Brie realized she must seem dangerous to Maura. Some dork who got good grades and had never French-kissed a boy had somehow bewitched HHS's golden girl, threatening to edge Maura into obscurity. When Lindsey ordered three drinks, Brie gave one to Maura.

"It's an amarello sour, I think," she said.

Maura ate her cherry and dropped the stem on the floor, then patted Brie on her heap of curls. "You're so clueless it's kind of cute."

Brie sipped at the sweetness in her glass. All she had to do was play dumb and Maura would forget to compete. She was surprised it had taken her this long to figure out. When Lindsey got her drink, they claimed a tall table.

"School is in session, hon," Maura said, pointing to the crowd. "Pick a guy."

"For you or me?"

"Me first, so you can watch me work," Maura said, running her fingers through carefully tousled amber waves. "Make him cute."

"What about Adam?"

Maura tipped her head, lips pursed as if Brie was a big-eyed beagle puppy. "Let me worry about him, okay?"

Brie smiled back. "The one with the hair in his eyes. Blue button-down."

Maura nodded. "Not bad." She plucked the cherry from Lindsey's drink and lifted it by the stem to her mouth. Her tongue darted out, tasting it as she glanced at the man in the crowd— mid-twenties by the look of him, chiseled face with the ghost of a smile—then she bit the saccharine fruit off its stem. The man licked his lips and pushed his way toward them.

"*Baila conmigo,*" he said, plucking Maura's free hand from her lap.

She sipped again before letting him pull her to the dance floor. "Man, I knew all that French was a waste of time," she whispered to Brie as he drew her away.

"I can't do that," Brie said, gulping her drink.

Lindsey laughed. "Sure you can. Look around, we can do whatever we want." Then Damian stepped through the entrance and Lindsey shot a desperate glance at Brie. "I wasn't planning on seeing him. I figured he'd work somewhere else by now."

"You don't have to hook up with him, you know," Brie said, watching the bouncer weave through the crowd. "We could just go back to the condo and watch stupid movies."

Lindsey put her hand briefly on Brie's. "Don't think I'm a slut. There've only been the two guys, as far as *that* goes, anyway. Tell me before he gets here."

"Behind you," Brie said softly, bending to sip through her red stirrer.

"I didn't think you could get prettier," Damian said, holding Lindsey by the chin. "But I see now I was wrong."

Brie bit her cheek to keep from laughing, but Lindsey closed her eyes and half-collapsed against his chest. "I was sure you'd forget about me," she said.

"Use your head," he chided, actually clucking his tongue. To Brie, his acting was worse than Shel's puffed-chest blustering as Prince Dauntless, but Lindsey seemed to buy it. Or maybe this was just the dance of people coming together. The fakery behind the fairy tale.

"I got someone to cover the rest of my shift," he said. "Let's go back to your place."

"I have to find Maura," Lindsey said. "And Brie needs company."

Damian glanced at Brie for the first time. "I'll take care of it," he said.

"That's okay," Brie said. "I have a book."

Lindsey laughed and gently shook Brie's arm. "You should do stand-up, I swear."

Maura and her guy had migrated to the far side of the dance floor. "We're leaving," Lindsey said, and Maura yanked her guy along.

Brie followed the four of them to the sidewalk, where goose bumps rose on her collarbone. Stumbling over her heels, she tried again: "Please, tell him not to call anyone."

"Too late, sweetie," Damian said, his elbow hooked behind Lindsey's neck.

"Brie," Lindsey called over her shoulder. "You need to get some action. You'll thank me later, I promise."

Brie's heart lodged in her throat. She thought of the stranger Damian had called, the boy who expected to drop in, get his rocks off, and disappear, on to the next. Worse, she could already see the way his face would freeze on seeing her—Cheese Pie, Limburger, the Funk. He'd try to mask his disappointment, whispering to Damian, "You really owe me, man." She knew she was expected to bear it the way she bore the listless conversations with boys at home while their friends made out with Lindsey in a poolhouse or by the carousel at the mall, but she was sick of it. She couldn't do it—flat could not—even one last time. She followed the group to the condo's lobby but told Lindsey to go up without her.

"I'm a little dizzy," she said. "I want to stay here and get some air."

"By yourself?" Lindsey asked, eyes narrowed as if watching the lie swirl between them.

"Sure," Brie said, forcing a smile. Maura's guy nuzzled her neck like a boar digging for truffles. "I'll be up soon. Promise."

Lindsey's mouth opened and closed before Damian made the decision for her. "My buddy Joey's on his way. You can bring him up."

"Really, you should tell him to forget it, go home. I'm exhausted," Brie said, but they were already filing into the elevator, all tongues pinkly visible between hungry lunges. It made her sick. Maybe she was naïve, but she didn't want some meathead named Joey to deliver "action" as a favor. She didn't want to massage Maura into a friendship, and if Lindsey thought she was joking when she was being sincere, then they didn't know each other at all.

Brie faced her reflection in the plate glass window, caught in the rush of a teeth-gritting anger. She hated this stupid tube dress and the drinks that tasted like candy but filled her head with static. She walked toward her reflection until she could see through it to the ocean. It was the same Atlantic she'd grown up with, but down here it adorned itself with big rolling waves and white-sand beaches fringed by plastic-looking palm trees. Even the ocean in this pastel-plastered tourist trap was just another whore.

Brie wanted to call up Katrina and ask her how she knew so much about animal mating habits. She wanted to go back to that Halloween party and ask the Cereal Killer to dance. She wanted to stand behind the counter at her father's shop and give wrong directions to tourists en route to the Kennedy compound. If she could find a way home, she'd work for free all summer and watch the kids and never complain, so long as she could be her mousy self in peace.

"Are you Bea?" The voice was uncertain, reedy. She spun at the window where the dark ocean had hypnotized her.

"I guess you're Joey," she said.

He was thin, black, wearing khakis and a blue polo shirt with a logo over his heart reading "Dan's Parasailing." Not the bruiser she'd expected. Still, he must expect something of her to have come on such short notice.

"Sorry, this is awkward," he said, a smile materializing and then snapping out of sight.

"It is, isn't it?" she said, letting herself laugh. It *was* awkward. And so was Brie. She had let Lindsey believe they were alike because it was flattering to think it was true. In the morning, she'd tell her she wasn't a project to be made over. She was just Brie and always would be. Then she'd call her father and beg him to wire money for a bus ticket north.

"You didn't have to wait," he said. "I've been up there before."

Of course. For last year's third wheel. "You go up. There's probably still some booze."

He dug his hands into his pockets and leaned back against the streetside wall. "I bet it's safer down here. Last time, D's girl put a pizza in the oven and passed out. Everyone else was so wasted they slept through the fire alarm. I saved their damn lives," he said, shaking his head with a rueful twist of his lip.

"What leftover did Damian call you to console then?" she asked, then couldn't stop herself from going on. "Do you even remember her name?"

His jaw dropped as if she'd slapped him. "It was just a party," he said, slowly, cautiously. "There were twenty people up there. What kind of a loser do you think *I* am if D only calls me to entertain 'leftovers'? We had plans after his shift, and then you all showed up—no, you know what?" He held up his hand. "Nice to meet you. Have fun in Laudy."

She let him swing the door open to the sea wind before she called his name. "Look, I'm sorry. I told him not to call anyone for me. I don't do—whatever people do down here."

"You sure about that?" he asked, raising his eyebrows in a way that made her turn to face her reflection again. In the glass, she was a party girl named Bea who had never been called Limburger, or sat on the sidelines of a 4-H Halloween Dance. Tonight, if she wanted, she could take the stage instead of haunt the wings. But what was the point? Soon enough she'd be home, back in her own skin. The door let a constant, whipping ocean breeze into the lobby. She stepped out of the heels and bent to pick them up in one hand.

"My name's Brie, and this isn't my dress. None of this is me," she said, with a flourish of the borrowed shoes. "You seem nice, but you don't have to stay."

He regarded her from across the foyer, adding her up like a math problem, before letting the door close them back in. "I am nice," he said, deadpan, before cracking another smile. "And believe it or not, I'm about more than parties."

She felt something loosen in her chest. "Okay, then," she said, reaching up with her free hand to unclip her piled curls against the headache born of their weight. "What are you about?"

"School up in Gainesville. Go, Gators!" he said. "Summers I drive a Chris-Craft down here. Tourists let me strap them into harnesses and fly them like kites. I watch horror movies. Play piano. What about you?"

"At home, I rent bikes. My dad has a shop. It's all tourists, Memorial Day to Labor Day. I bet we've met the same ones. The guy who won't take his sunglasses off inside. The lady who calls everything 'quaint.'"

"The kid dripping ice cream like a breadcrumb trail," he said, nodding. "You ever tried it, though? Parasailing? I'll take you up. Gratis. It's actually a decent rush."

"Now?" She hid one foot behind the other. "In the dark? Isn't that kind of dangerous?"

"Yeah, and the last time I went upstairs I could have burned to a crisp in my sleep."

Parasailing at night with a stranger was something Bea the party girl would do, but the idea of that scouring breeze, flying above dark water—it quickened her breath. The sweet tingle was back in the hollow of her stomach. Brie wanted to take that story back with her. Assuming she survived. Not all risks were created equal, after all. Some had to be worth taking.

"Let me get some normal clothes on," she said, punching the elevator's "up" button. Her heart had turned hummingbird. It wasn't a good idea, probably. Maybe it was flat-out stupid. But she did want to fly that way. To surprise herself. To walk out on a limb of her own choosing. "Want to come up?" she asked. It wasn't a test, not really, but she didn't fight the relief that trickled through her when he said he'd wait downstairs.

"I'll just be a minute," she said as the doors opened.

"Brie, check the oven," he said. "I'm being real. We don't want that on our conscience."

We. She savored it, and said she would. The condo was littered with empty glasses. Laughter came from behind one of the bedroom doors. In the bathroom, Brie shed the skin of her borrowed dress and slipped on jeans and a pink T-shirt she'd brought to sleep in featuring the starship *Enterprise*. Grabbed a bulky gray sweatshirt.

After inspecting the oven—empty, cold—she stepped onto the balcony at the same height to which Joey's harness would propel her, taking in the same spread of twinkling lights that would blur below her flight path like stars. She closed her eyes as the wind battered her sticky jumble of curls, and when she lifted her hands from the railing, she already seemed to be flying.

Acknowledgments

So many people helped bring this book to life. Thanks to the faculty, staff, and students who welcomed me to ASU and FSU, especially those of you who read these stories and made them better in class, beneath buzzing desert halogens, while swatting mosquitoes on Black Dog's patio, or over the phone with too many miles between us. Special thanks to the teachers who helped me turn first drafts of these pieces into finished ones: T. M. McNally, Julianna Baggott, Melissa Pritchard, Mark Winegardner, and Elizabeth Stuckey-French. I fill my own classrooms with your collective wisdom.

Over the years, I received funding to attend the New York State Summer Writers Institute and the Sewanee Writers' Conference, where I was grateful for the encouragement of Lee K. Abbott, Binnie Kirshenbaum, Margot Livesey, and Randall Keenan. The wonderful Marina Merli made space for me at the Arte Studio Ginestrelle for three unspeakably beautiful weeks in Umbria where some of these stories were edited. Thanks to Texas Tech University for travel and research support, and to my colleagues whose work and support heartens and astounds.

I'm indebted to Lisa Williams for selecting the manuscript and for her keen editorial vision that sculpted from those pages a leaner, better book, and to everyone at the University Press of Ken-

Acknowledgments

tucky, particularly Patrick O'Dowd for his superhuman patience and Ann Marlowe for her perspicacious and inspired copyediting. Special thanks to the editors who originally gave the stories homes, especially John Wang, Matthew Limpede, Sam Ligon, Jennifer A. Howard, Odette Baker, and Barry Kitterman at *Zone 3*, who was the first person to make room in the world for my words.

Thanks to my early readers and those of you who've variously saved the day with Skype dance parties, three-hour dinners, copious margin notes, and always excellent advice: Marian Crotty, Caitlin Horrocks, Todd Kaneko, Matthew Gavin Frank, Douglas Jones, Leslie Jill Patterson, Dennis Covington, Shannon Reynolds, Shannon Ventresca, Jen Wright, Elizabyth Hiscox, Beth Staples, and Elizabeth Weld.

Love and gratitude to my family and my parents for everything, but especially for sharing their passion for reading—and for lending me their books; and to my brother, Anthony, for cheering me on and letting me play *The Sims* in his room until all hours, which was really a way of writing these stories, even then.

To my son, I love watching your story fill in. You are the best thing I've ever made.

And to Robby, thank you for your insight and intellect, for cracking me up and keeping me afloat, and for all you are to Milo, and will be. This book wouldn't exist without you.

THE UNIVERSITY PRESS OF KENTUCKY
NEW POETRY AND PROSE SERIES

This series features books of contemporary poetry and fiction that exhibit a profound attention to language, strong imagination, formal inventiveness, and awareness of one's literary roots.

SERIES EDITOR: Lisa Williams

ADVISORY BOARD: Camille Dungy, Rebecca Morgan Frank, Silas House, Davis McCombs, and Roger Reeves

Sponsored by Centre College

 CENTRE
C O L L E G E